Don't let go

by

Leah Sin

ALL THINGS ENGLISH

I've decided, as I embark on this new adventure, that I'm done with doing what my parents and family ask of me; I've obeyed for long enough now, even when I didn't 100% agree. I toed the line and followed the advice.

I've learnt from the receiving end of judgement that I have no right to it and it seems my new personalised way of thinking freaks a lot of people out, men especially. Which I'm grateful for at the moment, I'm hoping it will keep trouble at bay. Fresh start and all.

My sister likes to call me 'safe' but I would be quick to argue that it's, considerably, as a result of her making it her life's mission to shock the shit out of our very middle-eastern, super conservative mother. Thereby making anything I do scrutinised with the same intensity.

Akia is 6 years older than me and to say that she hit the floor running the day she finished school would be an understatement. She chose the night that she got her results to announce, to our entire family, that she secretly applied to a university overseas and had been accepted.

This was bad enough but then she creamed the cake by coming out. My mother *loved* Leila until Akia confessed that she wouldn't be leaving without her. My mother had gone on about how close they were until my aunt explained. Then...well then she had to be escorted to her bedroom to lie down, so severe was her shock.

My younger brother, Tariq, and I disappeared into my bedroom to avoid the pending shit storm but the celebration came to a sharp halt following Aki's announcements. Family members literally hauled ass out and soon we were confronted by our bewildered father.

He couldn't understand what all the fuss was about (Bless him and his very liberal upbringing.) Aunty Soula snuck in and gave him the rundown on what was considered unacceptable behaviour within the adult female Arab community; it was both hilarious and cringe-worthy! I was equally impressed with and curious about my aunt's knowledge.

Dad was adopted out of a Persian orphanage by an American couple and had lived all over the world with them. (I LOVE my American grandparents and am so grateful for them!) My parents met while my dad was doing his post-grad in Egypt and they've been together ever since.

He travelled a lot when we were younger but there was always an aunt or two around so Akia, Tariq and I grew up surrounded by laughter and strange traditions. We lived for trips to America and were lucky enough to spend time in some amazing countries because of dad's archaeology.

Of the three children, I'm the only one that didn't get a traditional name; my dad claims it's because mom named Akia so it was his turn next. Tariq used to tease me that it was because our mother wanted a son and when I arrived she wasn't bothered with my name. The jackass, if only he knew!

So anyway that's how I landed up with Amarelia. Of all the western names or even Eastern names, he could have gone for...he chose Spanish Amarelia. He loves to tell that I was born under a full moon and therefore was his child of the moon.

I swore Tariq to secrecy (the childhood dirt I'd collected on him probably helped) and all through school I managed to get away with Lia Wolfe. Mom had a word with my class teacher every first day of the year. Tariq says it's her penance for allowing our father to name anything, especially a child.

Now though, as I filled in the paperwork, I knew I'd have to come clean. My stupid passport had my full name on, **Amarelia Said Wolfe**, thanks for helping dad! Everyone made the same joke (why did Ameralia say wolf?) ha de ha. Begrudgingly, I filled in the lines and handed my stack of papers over to the school bursar who doubled up as HR it seemed.

She was a very orange, very chatty woman with a thick scouse accent. I was directed to where I'd be living for the next few weeks until my transfer into permanent digs and I practically skipped along the tree-lined path. Everything looked like a fairy tale, I felt as though I was in a film set.

The university was so beautiful and I was so grateful that I got picked to do my post-grad here. Mr Callen came to my University in Madrid and gave a few guest lectures. I instantly knew that I wanted to absorb all the memory out of his head.

He's the leading professor in England on all things mystical and the only reason my mother FINALLY agreed to allow me to apply was my father telling her about Mr Callen's extensive research into Kabbala and the Surah's. Both of which my mother poured over every chance she got.

Professor Callen only accepted a maximum of 3 students a year as researchers. The essay I had to write to get considered took me three months and five do-overs before it felt ready. When the response letter finally arrived I was too nervous to open it and almost retched when dad teared up.

Our house was a flurry of motion for weeks after my response. My mother went into prep over drive. You'd swear I was moving to Siberia, not England. Tariq had to book me a ticket to visit during the break to calm her down. Suddenly she cared?

Akia sent a parcel from her and my grandparents before I left; she had relocated permanently to the States two years before, with Leila, and was so happy that our mother had come around...mostly.

I was warned my room would be small so Tariq agreed to stash the XL suitcases my mother forced on me at his place. I was excited to buy a new wardrobe. Most of the clothes I wore in Spain (where we'd been living for the past 6 years) wouldn't cut it in England's climate.

Once I'd transferred my worldly possessions into a tiny closet I made my way straight to the closest high street. I needed an Argos and a Poundland ASAP. I also needed British clothing stores. I've always loved how the English dress. You could be a knee-high boot, short skirt wearing kick-ass chick one day and a romantic floral princess the next.

I got lost trying to find my way around the campus when I got back and realised that instead of shopping maybe I should have spent my first afternoon getting to know the grounds better.

JACKASS

I met him by accident - literally! I was about to cross the road when he just about mowed me down on his bicycle. He swerved at the last second to avoid the gigantic pothole in front of me. The roadworks sign had fallen over, making the hole a surprise.

Granted my overzealous screech did cause him to wobble and crash, head first, into a bench but he came so close to knocking me down that it was out before I could shut my mouth. I sidestepped the hole and rushed to help him gather the plethora of paper sheets and books that had exploded from his satchel.

It happened exactly like in the movies; we reached for the same book but instead of being a moment we bumped heads. He scowled at me and ripped the book from my fingers. I had to bite my lip hard not to laugh. He was so irate that I could see a thread fine vein pulsing in his neck.

I'm a nervous giggler and I get worse the better looking the guy is. This one was gorgeous, in a threatening almost hostile way. Everything about him was big and scary, like a lion. He had the straightest nose I've ever seen with big hazel eyes and a mane of chocolate and honey hair. The beard was er hmm very good. He was unsettlingly handsome.

"I'm so sorry; I wasn't paying attention to the road." I decided to be magnanimous. "Yeah obviously, do you always wail like a banshee when a bicycle passes you?" He bit out. "Well, you didn't seem to notice the gaping hole in front of me either. If I'd stepped out you would have landed on me in the hole instead of the bench." I hissed back at the jerk but he was trying to get under his sleeve to his watch.

"Agh now I'm going to be late. Just stop, stop jumbling my stuff up, leave it." "Oh whatever, you are a completely rude jackass, here!" I chucked the papers I held at him and swivelled as I stood.

"Did you just call me a jackass?" He called behind me and I heard him laugh quietly. "I did, a completely rude jackass," I called over my shoulder and carried on marching. Thanks to the jackass I'd forgotten why I was jaywalking in the first place, I was late!

The echo of my footsteps rang around me as I double-timed it toward the hall. I stopped to ask for directions and when I slid in I was met with deafening silence and the stares of about 50 students.

"Miss Wolfe, welcome. Thank you for joining us at this early hour." Mr Callen sang sarcastically. He had an annoying habit of tapping his pointer on the desk when he was upset and I gathered from the staccato it rapped out now that he was pissed.

"Sorry Mr Callen I got lost and almost run over," I explained while my ears burnt from embarrassment. Sniggers rippled through the hall and I wished I could start again, this was not the impression I wanted to make.

"Was your assailant tall dark and handsome perchance?" "I...suppose?" I followed his gaze to a side table and groaned internally when my eyes landed on the jackass.

"You flatter me but I didn't almost run you over. You yowled like a drowning cat and made me face plant a bench." "I explained the hole and I apologised. You didn't have to be-." "A completely rude jackass?" He finished for me but I didn't miss the smirk. That earned another wave of giggles. Mr Callen laughed deeply.

"I retract any earlier resentment on your tardiness Miss Wolfe. Anyone who can get away with calling Mr North a completely rude jackass and live to tell about it deserves a reprieve. Please take a seat alongside him, he'll catch you up."

Prof Callen instructed and I didn't miss the way all eyes slid to the assistant's table while he narrowed his eyes at his teacher. I didn't trust what would come out of my mouth so I nodded and made my way over grinding my teeth with each step.

What started off as humiliating ended in fascination and awe. Callen Is possibly the most knowledgeable person I've ever met and his lecture totally sucked me in. I managed to ignore my partner through most of the class by making notes and asking questions. As soon as the class was over I made my way down to the professor.

"What did you think of your first lecture Miss Wolfe?" He asked me over the head of another student. "Fascinating! I was actually wondering about the Rose meridian." I started but was cut short when the Prof was summoned by another lecturer. As he excused himself he told me to speak to Rawk about the meridian.

"Who's Rawk?" I asked after him but he was gone. I dropped my hands on my thighs enjoying the sting when they connected. "I am," Jackass said from beside me with a quick uneasy smile. "Oh." "Look about earlier it's just the Prof doesn't tolerate lateness and I'm trying to stay on his good side this year."

"This year? I thought he only had postgrads in lecture?" "He does usually, I'm an exception. I was one of his postgrads last year but I had an um well let's just say I had a bit of a rough episode at the end of the year."

"Oh okay well I'm going to get something to eat I'm starving and I need to be back for the second session so I'll see you around?" "Yeah sure, later." "Later." I gave him a weak wave

"Hey, I don't know your name." "Ama...Lia everyone calls me Lia." "What's your real name?" "It's weird." I scrunched my nose at him and the corner of his mouth flicked up for a moment. "I doubt that." He cocked his head to the side.

"Amarelia," I confessed. "Amarelia's pretty, better than Lia." He flashed me a half-smile and disappeared into the leaving crowd, scowling at a girl who bumped into him as he walked. I stood rooted to the spot for a few seconds blinking, what just happened? Had the completely rude jackass turned into a prince charming in front of me?

All through the second session, I had to remind myself not to stare at Rawk. I wasn't into him rather more interested in him. I wanted to know what had happened last year and why the Prof had given him a second chance, I heard he never gave second chances. I had taught myself not to seek involvement but Rawk was such an itch and I really wanted to scratch.

After the session, Callen gave us our first lot of research to complete. I looked at Rawk with eyes like saucers, there was so much! At least I could assure my mother that I wouldn't be going to crazy parties or meeting frat boys, I would never be finished researching!!!

"I know it looks like a lot and it is but from the questions you've been asking I think you'll enjoy it. Come on no-one goes to the library at this time we should be able to get through a fair amount if we work together yeah. " He made it sound like more of an order than a request.

"If we work...oh yeah okay." I didn't know how to be around him yet, I found him particularly difficult to read so I chose to go with the flow. We walked to the library in silence but I noticed a few people staring and whispering.

"Don't mind them." He followed my eyes. "What's that about?" ", some people feel I shouldn't be here." "What *did* you do?" "I fucked up." He answered quite aggressively startling me. He clenched his fist and jaw when he noticed me hesitate.

"I'm sorry." I stepped apart from him and felt my face flood with colour. "No, I'm sorry it's just I don't want to talk about it." "Okay." I sat on the other side of the desk with a million questions bumping around my head but the fierceness I had seen flash in his eyes stopped me from trying to ask.

PINKY PROMISE

We worked well together and by the time we called it a day I was beside him whisper laughing at his ridiculous impression of an American accent. "That's awful!" I teased him and he hissed at my silent hysterics. "I'm much better after a couple of drinks." He assured me. "I'll take your word."

"You don't have an accent; your voice is just melodic." I wasn't certain how to take that, "Thank you, I think. Hey, may I ask a personal question? Non-Uni related." I added when I saw him clam up instantly. "Okay."

"What's your heritage? You have incredible features but they definitely cannot be purely English." "That is the last thing I was expecting you to ask. I have quite a mixed family tree. My father's Welsh. My mom was half Japanese and half French."

"It's a great combination." I ran my eyes over him like a pervert. "Are you saying you find me attractive?" "Oh God no I mean you are it's just I wasn't saying hmm I'm sorry I'm going to leave now before I totally embarrass myself."

"It's alright it's actually great to be around someone who isn't saying what they think I want to hear or hasn't chosen to believe the rumours about last year or my family or okay now I'll stop." He laughed but I heard the hostility under it.

"I'll um see you later." I was halfway out of my chair already, desperate to get away from the mix of fascination and fear he made me feel. "Amarelia are you in permanent Res yet?" he called behind me and I had to swallow hard.

The way he insisted on using my full name and the way he said it was quite spine-tingling. "Um no I'm not yet; I'm in Blythe House for the moment." "That's the other side of the campus, here let me walk you." He jumped up and took a pile of books from me.

"Oh no, you don't have to." "Please I insist." "Um okay, thanks." A stray giggle escaped and I jammed my lips together to stop any others from getting ideas. "Nervous giggler?" he asked, "I am." Colour flooded my face yet again and I wished I could get sucked into the ground.

"Do I make you nervous?" He asked with a frown. "Yes." Screw it why not be honest? "Why?" His tone suggested that he didn't really want to know the answer. "You're very good looking." "My face makes you nervous." "Egh no that's not what I mean."

"So you don't think I'm good looking?" "Yes, you are that's not what I-. It's not your face that makes me nervous; it's the flashes of anger in your eyes. I'm sorry that sounds so rude it's not-."

"Amarelia stop its okay I get it. You feel the hostility in me." "Yes, the hostility that's it." "And that makes you nervous?" "Very." I was honest. "Why?" "It makes me uncertain of how to act around you, of what I can and can't ask or do. That reminds me of a time I'd rather forget"

"You make me nervous too you know." He looked like he wanted to discuss the times I would rather forget so I pushed on, "WHAT, me, how?"

"You're very honest." He murmured "Honesty is a bad thing?" "No it's a very foreign thing and it makes me nervous to hear what comes out of your mouth. The lies I'm prepared for." "Would you prefer me to lie to you occasionally?" I was teasing but he considered it seriously for a few seconds

"No, I actually think it will be good to have someone around who is totally honest with me." "Absolute honesty it is then." I grinned widely when he held out his pinkie to me. "Promise?" "Promise," I answered solemnly. I didn't foresee a reason I'd ever have to lie to him. He laughed deeply and kissed our pinkies.

"Your promise has been sealed with my kiss so you can never break it." He smiled wickedly at me. "Pretty sure it's meant to be a different type of kiss." I teased. He ran his fingers through his beard before leaning in and kissing me softly on the cheek. It was so close to my lips, I was shocked and thrilled by him.

"Better not break your promise now." He rumbled into my ear "I don't see why I'd ever have to lie to you." My voice was shaky at best. "Give it some time, you hardly know me yet."

His sentence had a bitter edge to it and I wished I could ask him what had happened to make him so jaded. Instead, I smiled quickly and we walked on in silence. This guy had so many sides to him. I tried to reconcile them as my mind raced.

"I'm sorry." He burst out and I jumped "For what?" "I can hear myself being short with you one minute then trying to be normal the next. It's just become easier to be defensive. Tell me I'm being a twat when I do it okay?"

"Okay." We arrived at Blythe House and I stuck my arm out to take the pile of books he'd carried. "Thank you Rawk, I'll see you tomorrow morning." "Yeah, bye Amarelia." He shot me a smile but his eyes stared me down with confusion in them.

"Are you into Rawk North?" A girl I didn't know asked when I walked through the front door. "What no I'm the new researcher for Prof Callen." "Oh good, he's the type you stay far away from, trust me, I was here last year and trust me-."

"Look I don't know what happened with Rawk last year but I also think that it's up to him to tell me about it so thanks for your concern but nothing is happening between us." I cut her off and marched to my room.

I ached to know what had happened. I spent the evening wondering if I could find anything in the library and if that was wrong? I thought maybe I could just outright ask but then I remembered how angry he'd gotten at just the mention.

How bad could it have been? So he had probably made a fool of himself, gotten drunk and had a fight or damaged property. If it had been any worse there's no way he'd be back here this year, right???

TAKE ME TO CHURCH

The next weeks were a blur of research and coffee. I'd been warned that Callen was a slave driver but damn! By Friday I couldn't see straight. Rawk walked me to Blythe House every day and I was more than grateful, there was just so much to carry and it was so far. Plus I got drip-fed bits and pieces of his personalities. I noticed how certain people got different versions of him, I was completely mesmerised.

"Thanks, Rawk, I'm so glad I get to move closer soon." I really really was. "Where did they put you?" "In Cossick House." "Much better for my poor arms." Rawk smirked when I rolled my eyes at him.

"Yeah, mine too. Thank you for helping me and for walking me." "It's nothing, I don't mind." "Well, I'm grateful anyway." "Have a good weekend Amarelia."

"I plan to sleep for most of it. Please tell me you are as exhausted?" "I've already done this for a year, remember, but yeah I'm knackered. I reckon I'll try sleeping tomorrow day away then off to church."

"Seriously? I never pictured you as a churchgoer?" "What does a church-goer look like exactly?" He raised his brows at me. "I'm sorry you're right that was rude." "It's not rude. You're allowed to have an opinion. Don't you go to church?"

"Oh wow um religion is a very touchy subject in my household. I'd need hours to unravel it to you." I exhaled loudly at the thought of my family's strange love-hate relationship with the various Gods.

"Have you ever been to a catholic church service?" "When I was much younger, yes. Not as an adult." "So what religion do you practice, if any?" "I don't I guess. I mean I don't doubt that there is something more than me out there but."

"But you can't say that spending time between any four walls makes you more Godly." "Something like that. It's more of a mixed upbringing thing in my case." "Mixed how?" "Hmm, that's another long detailed conversation." I laughed out.

"Maybe you could explain it to me one day?" He shot a guarded look at me for a second. "Um sure." I smiled and he returned the look. "Goodnight Amarelia." "Goodnight Rawk."

I turned to walk in but he called out to me, "Wanna come to church with me?" "Me?" "Yeah, for research sake?" I shook my head and shrugged. "Why not, where and what time?" "I'll come to fetch you tomorrow at 5 yeah." "Okay."

He arrived just before 5 looking like a totally different person. "Hi, you look good." "Yeah you too, you should wear dresses more often."

His eyes blazed a trail from my head to my toes. The dress was nothing much, a stone coloured knit dress. I had paired it with boots and a calf-length coat. "Oh um, it's one of only two I own at the moment but thank you. It's my mission to accumulate a killer wardrobe whilst here." "Well, you are off to a very good start." We walked to his car chatting about research.

"Got a new one North? Try not to damage this one like the last one." A guy called from across the road, within a group outside Collin House. "Fuck off." Rawk shouted back and yanked my door open. "Get in." He ordered and I did as I was told immediately.

I really wanted to ask but I could see from the fine vein pumping in his neck that it would not be a good idea. The brave mouse broke away from his buddies and started walking toward us. My eyes were huge when I turned to Rawk.

"Is he coming to pick a fight with you because I am going with you?" I asked quietly. "He's a fucking bell-end and I should have done worse to him when I had the chance. This won't take long." Rawk looked livid as he swung out of his car.

I had to stop this, one on one I had no doubt Rawk could take the guy on but if his buddies joined he wouldn't last long. Rawk leaned against his bonnet and crossed his arms allowing the guy to come over to him.

I could see the humiliation and rage brewing on the approaching guy's face. He came in close to Rawk and they had a very low, very urgent conversation. Both had their fists clenched at their sides, waiting for the opportunity.

When I saw the rest of the group making their way I snapped out of my daze. I scrambled out and walked around the car. I tried to look as innocent as possible.

"Hello boys. I'm sorry I don't know what this is about but Rawk here is my ride to church and I really can't be late. I'm meeting my daddy there, he's a visiting police chief and he hates when I'm late." I pulled out my best Southern accent and hoped the muscle would catch my drift.

"Ben leave it, he's not worth it." The biggest guy of the group sank a hand into Ben's shoulder then wrenched him away from Rawk. "This isn't over North; you're lucky she saved your ass." Ben hissed as his friends walked him back to Collin House.

Rawk tried to push past me but I caught him by surprise when I laughed out loud. "Oh sweetie no, I saved *your* ass from *him*. Let's be real for a minute." My sweet Carolina accent was replaced with pure Harlem.

I looked Ben up and down and then turned to Rawk and did the same. I heard a few sniggers and chuckles from within his group. Beside me

Rawk shook his head with a smirk, he was breathing hard to control himself.

I turned and got back in the car then buckled up; holding my breath while he decided what to do. I exhaled deeply when his long fingers wrapped around the steering wheel. "Thank you." He slid his eyes into mine for a second then started the car.

"Sure, are you okay?" I answered a few seconds later. "Yeah and we aren't talking about it." He pointed between us. "Okay." My brows knitted together but I decided to let it go given what had just happened. "You wanna know what happened between us." The way he said it made it more of a statement than a question.

"Naturally curiosity has me wondering but not necessarily. Unless it will impact on my immediate future I am happy to know when and what you feel comfortable telling me." It was the truth and he knew it too because he was on his best behaviour for the rest of our time together.

The church was...interesting, there are so many rituals and readings involved. I loved the singing and the art that was all around us but it was more the calmness it seemed to give Rawk that intrigued me. I had so many questions but didn't want to ruin his good mood.

"So there's this after church market, the kids sell the stuff they make at Sunday school, you keen?" He seemed uncertain right until I smiled "Sounds perfect!" He held out his hand to me and I followed him into the church gardens.

"Oh my goodness, this is amazing!" I held a beautiful beaded necklace up to Rawk and he laughed, "You're such a magpie but it is a particularly good one. How much is it Emma?" He taunted me then turned to the cute little blonde girl and smiled widely.

She went an extreme shade of pink and held up 1 finger. "One pound for that, Emma what have I told you? Your work is worth much more than that." He seemed to know the girl well and laughed when she cringed.

"I agree, I say at least 3 pounds." "Sounds much more like it, now stop underselling yourself Em." Rawk handed her the coins before I could take out my purse.

"You didn't have to get that, thank you." I didn't think he would like me to make a big deal of it and I was right. He stared at me for a few seconds "I don't get you and it's fucking with my head but I like it."

I thought about what he said for a few seconds then ghosted my fingers across his jaw. "Okay." "Really okay?" "I told you Rawk, you can tell me whatever you need to and I'll always try being honest back so yeah okay. I understand what you're saying and I agree because the same right back at ya."

We drove back to Cossick House in comfortable silence and were almost there when Rawk tapped my knee. "You'll be here next weekend right?" "Yeah, why?" "Oh see now I don't think I want to tell you that information right now." He teased as he stopped outside my dorm.

"So unfair but okay, thanks for this it was really fun." "You are so weird, yeah it was fun. See you at the library after breakfast? Unless you wanna come run the field with me" He called out his car window, earning a high pitched laugh from me, "Hell nooo, sweet dreams Rawk." "I wish, goodnight Amarelia."

DOLLED UP

I turned the envelope back over; it was definitely addressed to me. Oh shit, it was addressed to me and had lain undiscovered beneath a pile of Cossack House mail.

Oh my god, I was invited to the Professor's Christmas dinner and ball. I had one day left to reply and three days until the event. OMG! I scrambled to fill in the reply slip and rushed over to the main office, placing the card directly into the secretary's hand.

I knew that if there was any hope of me actually going to the dinner I would have to get through a ton of research so I headed to my room and buckled down for the mother of all research sessions.

The morning of the dinner I flew around my room getting ready for my early start, grateful that my roommate had already left for her Christmas holidays. I spent a fair amount of my morning at the library printing out and copying my research. Around 2 pm my phone rang and I grinned when Rawks name flashed across the screen.

"Hey what's up?" "Hi, just wondering what you're up to and if you have any plans for later." "Well, by some miracle, I cracked an invite to the Prof's dinner." I tried not to sound too smug but I was just so excited I couldn't help it.

"Look at you fancy pants. They're not that great you know." He teased and I snorted across the line. "But I've never been, so humour me." "You're right, you will have a ball." He sniggered. "What are you up to?" I ignored his pun.

"I have a few options now but I really need to get through a shit ton more research before I put on my dancing shoes." "I'm at the library busy printing out," I admitted with a giggle. " I may see you later yeah?" "Yeah see you later." I felt a blush race across my cheeks when I thought of Rawk in a suit.

I turned in my research and sprinted back toward Cossack House. There were just over 3 hours until the dinner began if I stuck to a plan I could get there and manage to look halfway decent...I hoped.

Nicole Evers was leaning out of the big window alongside my dorm room door and talking to someone beneath her. "Hey girl what's up?" I asked as I passed her. "Meh same old thing, what are ya up to this eve?"

"Oh not much just got an invite to the Prof's dinner." I squealed and she fed into all my excitement immediately. "What? Oh my God, that's brilliant. You're a first-year post-grad researcher and you cracked a nod, damn girl! What are ya wearing?"

"I have a few options but to be honest I haven't truly thought it through. I was just going to dive in and hope for the best." I answered honestly and watched her face twist in horror. "No! Not at your first dinner. We need Blanca." She pulled out her mobile and typed furiously.

Blanca could be heard from across the common area and a few minutes later stood in front of us glowing in anticipation. "Oh thank God you're here, we have an emergency." "What kind of emergency?"

"She has to be at her first-ever Prof's dinner in less than three hours and she hasn't even planned an outfit." Nicole pointed at me and grimaced at Blanca. "Gawd 2 hours! I'll do my best, come let's start, you sit!"

"Honestly it's okay don't fuss, I'll be fine. I have a dress and believe it or not I do own makeup and a brush." "Oh honey child, the Prof's dinner is so much more than a simple ball and you'll have to show up in so much more than standard. Where's the dress?" She threw open my wardrobe and pulled out the three plastic-covered options.

Blanca held my face between her fingers and turned me side to side then announced that I'd be wearing the royal blue dress. "Um isn't that a little um little?" "Noooo." Blanca looked offended

"It's perfect; everyone on the faculty will know who you are after this dress." "Dunno if that's a good thing but okay let's run with it." "Also, I'm thinking that colour dress and her eyes make it easy." "Smoky eyes?"

"Super smoky and red lips." "Let's see the dress on first oh and hair, messy half-up?" "Perfect and she won't need to wash it." "High or low?" "Oh, tough one but I think with this back or lack thereof definitely high and soft." "I love everything, let's make a princess." They started tugging and powdering me simultaneously.

"What do you feel about long bangs?" Blanca asked with a pair of scissors poised before me. "Like I'll love the idea this evening and hate you tomorrow." "I can live with that." She was snipping before I could stop her then spun me around toward my dress.

"Oh, I just remembered I have a silk pashmina that would go perfectly." I slid it out and both girls clapped. "It's a beaut, no peeking yet," Nicole warned me as she draped the pashmina and discreetly pinned it in place. I winked my thanks at her.

The thought of everyone being able to see down to my diaphragm didn't thrill me but Blanca was from Rio and too much skin was not a term she understood. She spun me around and moved me forward.

"Now open." "You look gorgeous, we are so good!" Blanca looked like a proud mama. "Thank you guys you're both amazing, I look amazing!" "Wait until you take that scarf off, then they're gonna see amazing darling!" She shot me a devilish grin

"Jesus Blanca, let's go get a drink, you crazy woman." Nicole shoved her toward the door and I held my arm out. "Please take this and buy a round or two on me, as a thank you. I really appreciate it." "Oh, darling girl you are the sweetest thing." Nicole sang sweetly. They took my offer and went off.

I locked my door and set off through the grounds. Halfway I started doubting my decision. The dress was way out of my comfort zone, not because I was body-conscious but because it was made to get attention and I wasn't that type of person any longer. I also had more makeup on than I'd ever worn and what if I what if fell or...I shook my head, shit I was going to be late.

SPIN ME RIGHT ROUND

"Okay, Lia you can do this!" I repeated to myself as I entered the ballroom. "Your name please?" The herald asked as I reached the staircase. "Lia-" "Amarelia Wolfe and Rawk North." Rawk stood beside me looking like he'd just stepped off a runway. "You in a suit is a good thing." "And you look...like an alternate version of yourself." He kept looking me up and down in amazement. "Yeah wait until I take the pashmina off." I teased making Rawk's smile widen. Holy moly he's gorgeous!

"Miss Amarelia Wolfe and Mr Rawk North." Our names rang out around the ballroom below and hundreds of heads turned as one. Rawk sucked in a deep breath and offered his arm. "Shall we?"

"Please don't let go of me, I'm petrified of falling on my face." "I got you Amarelia, you don't let go of me." "I hope we're sitting close." "Fuck I didn't think of that." "I still don't know why Callen invited me, I mean you I understand but I'm new. Wait, what do you mean you didn't think of that?"

"I asked him to invite you, you deserve to be here." "What that's wow thank you." "You work so hard and you never complain. If I get to endure this shit show so should you. Besides, everyone here already believes that I only get invited because of my family. May as well make it fun right?" He leaned in close to say the last part and wiggled his eyebrows making me giggle.

"Miss Wolfe and Mr North, good evening!" "Callen." "Good evening Sir." "You two clean up well and you seem to be getting along better." He dragged his eyes over all the points of contact between Rawk and me.

Heat burst through me and I wished my arm would dissolve. Rawk's entire body tensed and I watched his jaw clench tightly. He was pissed. "Any idea how we find our seats, sir?" I asked the professor quickly "Mrs Clancy has the lists, excuse me." Callen spotted someone and dashed.

"You okay?" I asked, removing my hand smoothly. "Fine, fuckin dickhead." He growled at me. I flushed again but now from anger and confusion. He was so infuriating! One minute he was hot then the next cold. Again I chose to pick my battles and followed him to Mrs Clancy.

We weren't seated at the same table instead we sat back to back and I was miserable. Of all people, I got stuck next to Meghan Ladbrook. She made it abundantly clear within the first 5 minutes that she would much rather have Rawk beside her.

She took every opportunity to lean over and catch his attention. By the main course, I was well on my way to getting drunk and found that if I turned away from Meghan I could ignore her desperate flirting.

On my opposite side sat Damon Coleman, the new zoology teacher. He only arrived yesterday but by speeches, we were engrossed in conversation. I could feel Rawk's eyes burning holes into me and I didn't dare to turn around. I didn't need to look to know that he was pissed off but I had no idea why.

I was well and truly lubricated when the dance floor opened and didn't hesitate when Coleman asked me to dance. I hadn't danced in years and it was so much fun to not care or worry, to just be free. Two dances and a weird conversation later dessert was served and I swayed back into my seat.

As I finished my pudding I felt Rawk's fingers wrap around my arm, setting off fireworks under my skin. The sensation was delicious and I was still a bit tipsy so I curved back into him.

"Yes," I purred, forgetting I was supposed to be angry with him. "Enjoying yourself?" "Yeah, you?" "Not really." "Aww lighten up, have a drink." " I can't." "Okay then dance with me instead." I stood and whipped my pashmina off in one move.

Had I been more attentive I would have noticed the collective eyebrow raise around me but all I saw was Rawk swallow thickly and stand up. He shook his head and started steering me toward the balcony doors but I was in too good a mood to get a lecture so I took both his hands in mine and pulled him to the dance floor instead.

"Please for me, just one dance?" I thought for a second that he was going to walk away but he shook his head and held out his hand to me. "One dance yeah." He tried to sound stern but his dimple gave him away. "Okay." "That's quite a dress. You weren't joking earlier." "Thank you, not normally what I would choose." "It's a great choice."

When the song ended I threw my arms around his neck and pouted dramatically. "One more?" I asked through my lashes and he rolled his eyes. "Why not?" He twirled me out and back in. We made up stories about the couples we danced alongside and I couldn't get enough of his hands on me. What the hell was I doing? Nothing could happen between us, it would be a disaster when it went belly up and would ruin everything.

Pulling me in close, he spread his one hand out against the small of my back and held my hand to his chest with the other. I was so glad I wasn't sober. "I'm sorry about earlier Amarelia." "It's okay." In all honesty, I wasn't sure which part of earlier he was apologising for and I had long forgotten the tension. "No, it's not, you did nothing wrong." "So why were you angry then?" I ventured. "Prof believes there is something going on between us." "But there isn't." I shrugged.

"Yeah but he thinks there is." Rawk pressed. "So who cares?" "I do and you should." "Okay but I know the truth and so do you. It doesn't really matter what a University teacher thinks he knows about my personal life, why does it matter so much to you?"

Rawk stopped dancing and traced his fingers along my knuckles for a few seconds, just watching me. "What?" "You've never asked me to tell you what happened last year."

"I didn't think you wanted to." "I don't." "Then you shouldn't." "Yeah, I should, come on." He took my hand and led me back to the balcony doors. I wasn't so sure I wanted him to tell me anymore.

MUSICAL CHAIRS

He searched the floor before taking a deep breath and launching into speech, "Last year didn't start last year, it started in high school. It just culminated last year." He ran his hands through his hair repeatedly.

"You only have to tell me what you're comfortable with," I assured him, I could see how difficult this was for him but before he could continue the doors drew back and Mrs Clancy tapped her finger to her watch and attempted a one-sided dance.

"I think it's time for the faculty waltz." He bit out. "The what now?" This was news to me! "The faculty FUCK! Sorry, let's just go do this before someone has something to say about it and rumours start." He raged then forced his temper down and held out his hand to me. As we walked in the MC announced the dance and he squeezed my hand in his.

"Stay close and stay the fuck away from Damon." He said harshly but his grin didn't match his tone. I snort laughed at his overprotectiveness as he fitted his hands around me.

"Don't laugh at me you'll regret it." He teased. I was bummed that I still didn't know what happened but he was so contagious when he was happy it didn't matter.

I stuck my tongue out at him and he flung me out suddenly then reeled me back in against him. My stomach and heart lurched. "Careful Amarelia." He warned against my ear. "Of what?" I turned my face towards his and heard him suck air in.

"I take it back; maybe it's me who needs to be careful." "Of what?" I pressed, turning around in his arms to face him. When he spread his hands out around my waist I thought my body would melt into two halves.

"Danger and you are a dangerous woman." "Huh been called many thing but never a dangerous woman." We moved in slow sweeps around one another.

"May I cut in?" Coleman appeared and instantly I felt Rawk's anger bubble up. He squeezed my waist before letting go and stepping back. I began to shake my head no as Coleman was about to step in. Rawk snorted and his arm flew up.

"Nope, not gonna happen. I can't Amarelia, I'm sorry. Not even for the sake of good manners." He whispered to me then turned to Coleman, "If you lay one fucking finger on her I swear to God yeah I will rip it off and feed it to you. Now fuck off Damon before I cause a scene." He practically vibrated with anger he was getting so worked up.

"Rawk!" I hissed but Coleman didn't seem surprised, in fact, he seemed to be getting exactly the reaction he wanted. "Oh wait are you two secretly dating, naughty?"

"No!" We answered together. "Then what's the problem? Besides you're probably safer dancing with me sweetheart." He was openly baiting Rawk and it pissed me right off. Rawk took a step forward and people stopped dancing around us.

I stood in his way and put my hands on his cheeks. I would deal with his temper to stop him making another regret. "Please take me home. I really want to leave with you right now." I kept eye contact and my focus seemed to work on him.

He clenched his jaw under my fingers but his hands came back up around my waist and he squeezed, I knew I had gotten through to him.

"Yeah, I'll get you the fuck away from this nonce." Rawk said over my shoulder and I turned to see Coleman's face pale at the reference. "Yeah mate we may have been fucked up but she still told me all about you lot. Stay the fuck away from Amarelia or what I did the last time will be a scratch compared."

Rawk held his hand out and turned on his heel. I gripped it tightly as he pulled us through the crowds. I had to stop my nervous giggles when I thought of what we must look like to those watching our dramatic exit.

I replayed the scene in my head as Rawk drove me back to my dorm. "What's going on in your head Amarelia, talk to me?" "What did you do to him the last time?"

"Put him in the hospital." He spat out. "Did he deserve it?" "What? Um yeah, he fucking did deserve it and more." "Okay then." I turned and looked out the window.

"Okay, just like that?" "Rawk if your reaction is justifiable then all I can do is accept it, I wasn't there. Besides he was a funny guy until he told me he wished he was my underwear before pudding." I grimaced

"He WHAT?" Rawk fumed and slowed his speed. "Yeah, the twat." "What did you say to him?" "That it sucked for him because I'm not wearing any." I grinned widely at Rawk. "Jesus Amarelia! Dangerous woman fucking hell!" He shifted in his seat and laughed darkly.

"Thank you for bringing me back and for not hurting any-one tonight." "Sure, it was unexpectedly fun." "Even the part where you wanted to break Coleman's fingers off?" I couldn't resist. "Especially that part! Goodnight Amarelia." "Sweet dreams." I sang "Not usually but who knows maybe tonight?"

The days leading up to final Christmas clear out were insanely busy. Rawk and I found a flow that worked for us and we spent many many hours together in the library and at the coffee shop.

"Are you clearing out?" I asked as we crawled out of our last research session, exhausted and starved. "Nope, not a huge fan of Christmas or family." "Okay." "No lecture?"

"They're not my family Rawk and I don't really buy into Christmas. My parents and Tariq will be here this weekend then they're going to my grandparents and sister in the States."

"So you'll be here alone?" He checked "I guess, you?" "Yeah, I have so much research to get ahead of." "Do you do anything on Christmas day?" "I don't do Christmas at all."

"Okay." I nodded and smiled "How do you do that?" He threw his hands up. "Do what?" "Agree and not question or lecture." "It's not my place. People should tell you stuff because they want to not because they think they have to. If you want my opinion ask for it."

"You're weird." "Thank you, you're a bit of a dick." "Thank you, although I am far less of a dick around you believe it or not." "Well shit lucky me." I mock fanned myself.

"Hmm, that remains to be seen, See you at breakfast on Monday?" "Yeah, have a good weekend." "Enjoy your family." "Oh hun, you have not met my family." I chuckled as we took off in opposite directions. I was too hungry and too tired to process the conversation we just had but I knew it was one I'd have to go back to, why did he loathe his family so much?

RAWK

RAWKS POV

*I know that I come with a department store
worth of baggage and issues but I am slowly
learning that there is so much more to
Amarelia than her fucking incredible face.*

*I wanted to know everything and that took my
mind to a dark place. A cesspool of all the
mistakes and regrets I've made. I could not
allow my dick to drag her into my shit pool.
That wasn't entirely true though and I knew it.
It's more than her sex appeal; it's her effect on
me.*

*She makes me less of a prick and I like who I
am around her a whole lot more than I like my
douche default setting. My attitude has been so
bad for so long that it's become me.*

*Don't get me wrong in the beginning I craved
the freedom that the bad boy image gave me.
Guys kept their distance and I simply made
girls too uncomfortable or frustrated to stick
around. I didn't give a shit about any of it; the
girls were just things that I used when I had an
itch that needed scratching.*

*To be fair I was pretty sure almost all of them
had daddy issues in some way and I filled some
sort of weird desire. With Amarelia though I
don't only want to fuck her. I mean I definitely*

do want to fuck her, repeatedly if possible, but there's more to it. I want to know her.

I want more with her, fuck! She's so fucking sharp and weird but good weird, amazingly weird. The weird that has me researching the stuff she tells me about because it actually interests me.

I was so busy staring at her earlier that when she caught me it took me a minute to realise but I couldn't break contact. Her eyes trapped me. I was saved by a student walking in but for a little bit there I was threatening to drown.

I know I'm in deep waters but it's like watching a car crash, I can't turn away from her. I love it when she opens up about her family and her time spent growing up all over the planet. Jesus, I am proper fucked!

I almost told her about Carys and when I think about it I wish I had. I actually feel bad about her not knowing. Part of me knows it's because I wonder if she'll still speak to me after. I was a fucking asshole before, much worse than now and honestly, I wasn't ready for her to hate me yet.

She was going to be the one that got through. It was happening already and I didn't know if I was ready to fill the hole that was left by Carys in my heart. I needed to switch off, I headed to my dorm in a cloud of pent up emotions.

There were decorations and alcohol spread out along the sorority house lawn, God it was

*Final Friday already, this place was going to
be a ghost town soon. It's been a year already.
I could go to Wales but the anger was still too
raw inside me, no I was definitely staying here
for Christmas...so was Amarelia...*

On paper we made sense. We liked the same
things, got along (mostly) and had similar
views. It was just that temper! In a different
reality, had I met him out, I would have
thought that Rawk was hot AF but his mood
swings and dangerous edges would have sent
me racing for the exit.

Being forced to be with me has worn him down
some and as much as I didn't want to admit it, I
liked what I found under his dazzling beauty
more, he enchants me. With that being said I
knew that he and I in any sort of a relationship
was probably a bad idea so why couldn't I stop
thinking about the possibility of it? I rolled
over and dropped my face into my pillow.

Instantly my traitorous mind went back to him
during break earlier staring at me. I felt it and
when I turned to face him he'd kept eye
contact. All I could do was swallow down the
butterflies and grin like a twit.

His tongue swept across his lips as they curled
up then he looked away. He shoulder bumped
me and carried on writing when a student
walked into the room. The feeling his look sent
through me was quite a thing and I squeezed
my legs together tightly to try squash the
delicious thoughts from pricking up again now.

I picked up a book for the millionth time and tried to start reading but it was no use, I flung it across the room instead. There was no point I was too preoccupied to take anything in. The book connected with the wall and landed with a satisfying thump. *"Just like my life, a sad boring lump!"* I told myself in the mirror. God, I had to get a grip.

Rationally I knew that I probably felt so all over the place because of the roller coaster of emotions I experience when I'm around Rawk and the pressurised deadlines we are always under. Yes, he was gorgeous and smart and had a wicked...oh God stop Lia!

I grabbed my coat and walked myself onto campus grounds, I was not thinking about Rawk a second longer! My family would be visiting and I would watch movies all day for Christmas. I just had to get through the next few hours without thinking of him.

"Lia! Hey, babe you alright or what?" Nicole passed me on the commons and I was glad for the distraction. She's been scarce lately so I hadn't told her about the dinner. "Hey, yeah I'm good, you?"

"Grand babe so tell me everything no show me! Your phone hands it over." I laughed but did as she asked. She gawked and looked up with a fat grin. "I am damn good and Blanca is just-." "Blanca?" I offered "Exactly, if this whole Uni thing goes tits up I'll open a business with her. Hey, are you coming to the sorority Final Friday?"

"I have no idea what you're talking about." "So funny, it's the last house party of the year before final Christmas clear out this weekend and there is always free alcohol. After Sunday this prison is on lockdown, every year we try to go down in flames."

"I'm not so sure that's my thing and my family are visiting tomorrow." I started backing away but she pulled me into her side and shook me out a little, "Seriously you need to chill sister, come on you can come for a bit, one drink?" "One drink!" I clarified and she whacked my shoulder while steering me toward a throng of bodies on a lawn. Oh, I didn't know about this!

NIGHT & DAY

The house was loud and packed with drunken students. Nicole pushed a plastic cup at me and shouted something about a chugging contest; I grinned and gave her two thumbs up.

She spun us around and pulled me along. We came through the crowd and straight into one of those college party scenes you get in American films. The last of the Rugby and Football teams were having a drink off. I watched in horrified amazement as they sucked down cup after cup. "That's insane, they'll get alcohol poisoning."

 "This is nothing, Rawk holds the record. God, he could put it away when he was still fun." "How do you mean?" No one spoke about Rawk and I wanted to know more "I mean before everything got fucked. I'm getting another drink, you want another?" She disappeared before I could decline.

The noise was giving me a headache and squinting through the bodies I could see where Nicole stood as I squeezed my way along. She was talking to a beautiful dark-haired girl I knew was in the literature clique.

"Excuse me, hi I'm sorry to interrupt but Nicole I'm going to call it a night. It's far too loud in here for me and I only finished Callen's research today so I'm exhausted." Nicole pouted but it was the other girl's response to Callen's name that interested me.

"So you're Callen's other researcher." It was more of a statement so I figured that she obviously knew Rawk. I wouldn't jump to conclusions though. "Yes, I am."

"So has Rawk tried getting into your pants yet?" "Say what, NO!" Suddenly she wasn't so pretty any more. "Aww, I don't know if that's better or worse." She giggled loudly and was obviously very drunk but when I threw my eyebrows up at her she stopped short.

"He has hit on you though hasn't he I mean look at you. Oh of course he has. Can't help himself it's a genetic code in the fucking family. Don't say I didn't warn you."

She was leaning into me and the stench of sour wine and cigarettes was nauseating. Also, I was getting really pissed off with her; Rawk wasn't here to defend himself and I didn't know if it was okay for me to.

"Okay well, thanks for that; I really need to leave now." I cut her off and turned to make my way out but her stupid laugh followed me and I spun back around.

"He's never tried getting into my pants because he can actually have an intelligent conversation with me so sex is not my only use. He told me that he has fucked his way through a stream of girls and never gave a damn about any of them, sorry if you're one of them."

Before she had a chance to think of a response I was out of there. I heard Nicole howling with laughter and hoped that I didn't just fuck up severely! Fuck Rawk was going to be so pissed off with me!

All night I lay awake, wondering what trouble my big mouth had caused for me. Had I just pushed a wedge between us and made an enemy out of the dark-haired cow, or both? I groaned into my blanket

Oh, shit what if she was one of Rawk's exes. What if Nicole told Rawk a twisted version of what happened? Shit, this was not good and my family would arrive in a few hours. I had to speak to Rawk before anyone else did.

I condemned myself to hell for the hundredth time as I laced up my good as new trainers. I don't run, hell I hardly exercise. I'm what you call naturally stringy but I knew Rawk would be running the football fields. He did every morning and so I trudged down there.

Ever faithful, there he was and gratefully alone. I closed my eyes and took one last deep breath as I stepped out onto the field. He jogged up to me with a puzzled look on his face. Good God he is impressive.

"You're awake and you're here, why?" "Yeah, it's um can we talk?" "Sure but you'll have to jog and talk. I have a few more steps to go until I can quit yeah." He pointed at his watch. "Um okay."

We took off and I didn't know where to start. "You look like you're about to confess to a murder. If so I'll help you bury the body you don't have to be nervous to ask."

"Very funny but before I start I need you to know that I am really sorry and things just got out of control and I know I had no right," "What the fuck happened?" He didn't look so jokey anymore "Okay so I saw Nicole Evers last night."

"Nicky was at Final Friday, were you at Final Friday?" "Don't look so shocked, yes I was there but I didn't stay for long it was an alcoholic nightmare in there but that's not the point." "What is the point?"

"Nicole was with another girl who started getting mouthy about you." "Who?" "I don't know her name. She's beautiful, long dark hair and she's a lit major." I glanced sideways and thankfully Rawk stopped jogging. I was desperately trying not to faint from the shock of exercise. "Stretch with me and tell me the whole story from the beginning."

I told him verbatim what happened while trying to look at anything but him. "Wow, so you told Siobhan that I only shag girls I don't give a shit about."

"Well no not exactly I told her you never shagged me. Look I am so sorry Rawk, I was totally out of line but she was just being such-"

"A bitch?" He injected with a grin. "Yeah, a bit." Relief oozed out of me when he laughed loudly. "That's classic! Don't worry about Siobhan; chances are she won't remember anything about last night. She likes to chat shite when she's had a couple."

"So just Nicole then?" "Now she is a different story." "Yeah, she um she seems to know you quite well or at least claims to." "Nicole, Siobhan and I grew up in the same town." "Oh okay, that's good."

"Why good, wait did you think I shagged them?" "I thought possibly Siobhan until I spoke to her." I grinned sheepishly. "Good God no!" He looked appalled.

"That's quite a reaction." I giggled at his horror. "Siobhan and I are cousins." "Huh, no shit." "Yeah, unfortunately, through marriage." "So definitely no dating?" "NEVER!"

"And um and Nicole?" I asked quietly and he was about to answer when someone called his name and we both froze. "Am I interrupting your early morning couple's work out?" The guy called out as he neared. Rawk closed his eyes and swore repeatedly. "Who is that?" "That's Stuart!"

MY PEOPLE

"Who is Stuart?" I hissed. Rawk tugged me toward him and turned me around. He kept my fingers locked in his and mumbled into my hair, "He's the utter prick that is dating Siobhan. Let me handle this?" I nodded and turned my best smile toward the approaching prick.

"I thought she was talking drunken shit again but maybe not? You took a new lover North?" He didn't try to hide the fact that he was checking me out and I wanted to burst out laughing. Rawks fingers squeezed around mine. "Piss off this is Lia Wolfe and she's my research partner for Callen."

"Which is exactly where I should be on the way to, I want to catch him before he leaves the University, excuse me." I tried to step away but Rawk practically ripped my fingers off. "She's right Callen will be pissed if we miss him, sorry Stu we will catch up later." "I'll walk back with you." Stuart wasn't giving up until he had something to take back to Siobhan.

"I don't have time for this right now; I wasn't going back to my room anyway." "I just need a quick word on the way to the locker room then?" "His stuff is at mine." I blurted out then looked up at Rawk through my lashes. He was either comically shocked or having a stroke. I turned to Stuart and he looked as though he was practising his story already.

"Um yeah, stuff is my um my stuff is at Ama at hers so we'll catch up I'll see you um let's go." He snapped out of his trance and spoke in a stream of nonsense. Then literally frog marched me off the field, leaving Stuart grinning from ear to ear.

"Oh God that was bad wasn't it, I just fucked that whole thing up, I am so sorry." I really didn't want him to be angry with me. "No don't you didn't do anything it's just I've never had a girl cover um I need to go, see you later yeah."

And he took off, left me halfway to the change room and headed toward the woods that ran behind the tracks. I didn't know what to feel or how Rawk was going to be when I saw him next. Shit, my family were coming; I had better get a move on.

It only took a couple of hours before I wished my family would leave already so I could go back to my room and chill. They argued from the moment I opened my dorm room door. My mother was angry with aunt Soula over a recipe and clicked away at her phone mercilessly.

Tariq argued with our father because he wanted to trade in his almost new car for a convertible. They stopped briefly at the restaurant and then continued on to the hotel they had booked into. I was so relieved to get back to the dorm that I didn't register Siobhan until she came up behind me as I walked through my door.

"We need to talk." She stated before inviting herself in. "Please come in and make yourself comfortable." I sang sarcastically. "Fuck he does have a fucking type doesn't he?" she looked me up and down and shook her head. "What are you talking about?"

"You actually don't know? I was so fucked last night I thought Nicole and Stu were lying." "Know what?" "What happened with Rawk." "Oh my God seriously, I don't give a shit what happened last year, it has nothing to do with me!" I sounded pissed which was only half true.

"You should give a shit and Stu said he saw you two together this morning." "So?" I shrugged. "Rawk doesn't spend time with girls; he fucks them and forgets them. If you're starting something with him just make sure you know what you're getting involved in. Girls don't seem to survive Rawk. " She warned me cryptically

"Okay...but we're not getting involved, we aren't fucking and he can tell me what he wants when he is ready to with his own mouth." I crossed my arms over my chest and she raised her palms. There was a knock at my door and she said she had to go. "Don't say I didn't warn you." She whispered as I pulled the handle back and her face paled dramatically when Rawk cleared his throat before her.

My look of sizzling anger must have set him off because before I could get a word in he had Siobhan by the arm and moved her into the hall. I was so pleased that any remaining students weren't around to witness this. "What the fuck are you doing here?" He asked through his teeth.

"I was talking to Lia that's all." She answered too quickly. "You're such a fucking liar, what could you possibly have to talk to her about?" "You and I and our relationship," I answered for her and Siobhan flushed with embarrassment

"Whatever the fuck happens in my life is none of your business Siobhan or fucking Stuarts. You said if I stayed away from you and your people you'd stay away from mine and leave me the fuck alone so again why are you here?" I could see how hard he worked to control his temper, the vein in his neck pulsed along with his jaw.

"So she's your people now?" She cocked an eyebrow and I knew this situation was about to blow up. "Okay...know what, I am not in the mood for this and Siobhan I've told you how I feel about Rawk's past so please just leave." I stood between them and heard Rawk snort.

"I'm not trying to create problems." She said over my shoulder to him. He moved closer to me and for a second I thought he may push past and bolt but instead, he leaned into the space between us. "Siobhan Lia isn't my people." He started and she laughed out loud before sending me a pitiful look.

"She's my person, singular, now fuck off and slither back to your nest of snakes." He finished before turning and walking into my room. I was too stunned to say anything, I turned around and left her stood there with her jaw on the floor.

"Whoa, what just happened there? I don't think you convinced her that nothing is happening between us by calling me your *person*." "What, no it doesn't mean it's not like that." He said shortly

"What does it mean then?" I was more confused than ever about the guy and also more attracted to him. It was a dangerous combination. "It means your inner circle, the people you consider the closest to you." Doubt raced across his face for a second but the huge smile that broke out on my face wiped it away.

"So we're friends?" "Yeah I mean I speak to you more than I speak to any-one else here. You don't know all the shit that comes with me and you don't care and you're...cool I guess."

He raked his hands through his hair, messing it up and I itched to wind my fingers into it. His words were sweet and honest and I was being a horn ball. I smiled genuinely at him, "Thank you, I find you fascinating and am glad to be considered a friend." I offered him a drink and busied myself making it.

I reached up on the top shelf to get the coffee but it chose that moment to finally give way and I was forced to juggle its contents above me. Rawk slid in behind me and held the shelf up with one hand. He transferred bottles and jars with the other until I could place mine down.

I turned in his arms thinking he would move, forgetting that he was still holding the shelf. I looked up into his intense eyes and they darkened holy shit! He tugged behind me and the shelf sprang free from the wall. I gasped and instinctively moved forward. Rawks lips grazed across my cheek and he snapped back, dropping the shelf and bracket.

"I'll um I'll come to fix it tomorrow. I need to go." He moved toward my door. "Okay, hey what did you come here for anyway?" "Oh shit yeah. Callen says there's a big convention in Ireland; he suggested that since we are both staying we should go. The department will pay for everything."

"Okay, when?" I asked quietly and he looked ashamed. "I'm sorry about Siobhan and you did nothing wrong, I'm just having a really fucked up day. This is a fucked up time of year for me in general." "You don't have to apologise, you can tell me more about the convention tomorrow okay?"

He nodded and threw me a quick smile. "See you tomorrow, goodnight Amarelia." "Yeah sure, sweet dreams Rawk." I heard him snicker and mutter something under his breath.

FIRST TIME

I felt a buzz against my foot, which was propped up on the desk between a tub of ice cream and a stack of books. I was blasting *Ghostemane* so loud that the windows rattled. The only other stay-ins, besides Nicole, were on a level below and it was Christmas Eve so why not? I was on my third or fourth alcoholic milkshake and I picked up my phone gingerly.

Are you awake? I'm bored AF!! R

Making liqueur milkshakes, want one?" Lia x

Is the x meant to be a kiss? Why do you insist on using Lia and how many of those have you had? R x

Okay so I may be tispy a bit but I make them real good!!! Lia x <~ lol because my name is stupid and yes it's a cheek kiss and you sent one to me also.

Tispy hey? Your name isn't stupid, it's beautiful and it suits you. R x <~ because now I feel like I have to.

How can Amarelia suit anyone? Its weird lol Lia x

It suits you because it's beautifully weird like you. I can't come over but talk to me, tell me how it went with your family? R x

Okay, but it's a long story. A <~ better?

And so started an hour and a half text marathon between us. Eventually, I was sober and tired and we said our goodnights. I fell asleep with a grin on my face and woke up with butterflies under my skin.

My brother called and we actually had a decent conversation, their flight was early the following morning and they were heading out to the airport hotel in the afternoon so I agreed to meet them for breakfast. Tariq fetched me in his rental and the food made the entire mission worthwhile, it was *amazing*.

To be fair it may have been my slight hangover combined with hunger. I ordered some extras to take back to my dorm. "I'm heading out; I have to meet Mo in half an hour," Tariq announced. Our cousin Mo had moved to the UK a few years back and Tariq always tried to see him when he could. "How are mom and dad getting back?" "Pre-booked an Uber before we left."

"Oh great so I guess I'm walking back then, I won't be able to get a ride?" I couldn't believe that my walking all the way back alone in the cold didn't bother any of them at all, WTF? "It's not even far Lia, I can drop you off but it has to be now." Tariq offered. "No I have to wait for my take-home order, It's okay I'll walk." I glared at him momentarily.

"Who is all the food for?" My mother enquired. "Me, I have research to do and Uni is a ghost town," I explained. My phone vibrated in my pocket and I couldn't stop my smile when Rawk appears in a Christmas jumper the screen. I could currently only hear my conversations properly if I used the speaker so I tried to turn as far away from the table as possible.

"What are you wearing?" I asked as I answered. "'Tis the season to be jolly right and I may have lost a bet, you in?" He answered dryly. "No, but close by, my family are about to leave. The walk back should take me about 20 minutes."

"There's no fuckin way you're walking anywhere on your own, it's freezing out Amarelia. Are your parents having a laugh? Where are you? I'm coming to get you." Oh my God, that was heard loud and clear and although I was shocked to my core I was also insanely grateful. He confirmed that I wasn't being a brat. I gave him directions and paid for my order. Then went back to my parents at the table and hugged my dad. My mother looked about to burst.

"What?" I whined. "Who was that?" "My research partner." "Why is your research partner coming to fetch you on Christmas day, where are his family?" "He doesn't think it's safe for a woman to walk alone and I don't know mother, I share research work with him, not personal details." My answer seemed to satisfy her. We walked out to wait for their Uber shortly after.

I thought she was going to go into cardiac arrest when Rawk drove into the parking. Everything about him and his car visually screamed intensity and trouble. "That's your research partner?" I introduced him to *Ghostemane* and it pulsed out of his sleek ride now. I worked double hard not to grin at my flushed mother.

"Yip, thanks guys love you! See you in a few weeks yeah, love you." I called out behind me as Rawk pulled up and cut his engine. He looked up at me as I neared and I knew he was asking if he had to say hi. I subtly shook my head and made my eyes as big as possible, a fat smirk on my face.

He bit his lip and opened my door. The second the lock latched, the Triumph's engine and radio roared to life and we peeled down the road. I was so impressed by his commitment to my cause that I laughed long and hard.

"You should laugh all the time, it's a great sound." He grinned again and my heart melted into my shoes, he was so beautiful. "And you should smile all the time, it's a great sight." He rolled his eyes at me. I waved my take-home bag back at him.

"What's in the bag?" "The best bacon roll you will EVER consume, EVER!" "Bold statement." "I am willing to make it!" We made our way up to my room and as we turned toward my door Stuart came along down the hallway. "What the fuck is he doing here?"

"Shh, wait, I have a hunch because of something Siobhan said. Just hang on a minute, if I'm right he's going to-" We watched as he stood in front of Nicole's door. It swung open and after he did a quick left-right he ploughed into her as she yelped then giggled. My sentence hung in the air as we both gasped.

"Shit, I knew it." "How, what did she say, that is so many kinds of fucked up?" He shivered. "She said Nicole and Stuart were with her at Final Friday but he definitely wasn't there. He got the info from Nicole, not Siobhan and besides she was really really drunk. There's no way she would have remembered me and Nicole knows me.

"They probably put her to bed then hooked up." "Poor Siobhan." "What?" "Don't get me wrong I'm not adding her to my birthday card list but it sucks when you're being lied to. No matter how horrible or intrusive she is I still wouldn't wish it on her."

"See you really are a decent person, now let's go judge these piggy buns." He held up the bag and took my keys from me. I watched him open my door and my heart fluttered. I had to keep myself in check, I was quite certain I would be getting a phone call from my mother later. The dread ate at my stomach already.

He had to agree with me, they truly were the best. Rawk fixed the shelf for me and I got him to put another one up while I had the manpower. We watched Netflix and ate bad popcorn but it was the happiest Christmas I've had in years.

He told me about the convention and it sounded great so we agreed to go together. He left soon after and anxiety set in. I watched the arms work their way around my clock.

Finally, the phone rang and as expected my mother wanted to know everything about Rawk, she was furious that he hadn't gotten out of his car. She went on and on about my behaviour and staying away from bad boys and bad decisions. Eventually, I reached my cut off point.

"Okay, you know what mother I'm really not in the mood for your lectures right now. It is the biggest cultural holiday of the year and I am sitting on my own in an abandoned school. I have no family and no friends around me and the only person that *is* around and *is* my friend *is* Rawk. So please just get off my back and his case. You know nothing about him so stop judging him."

"I'm not judging, I don't want you to get hurt again." "God nothing is happening between us. We have been advised not to get involved because relationship problems mess with research. Besides if anything did happen it would be my mistake to make mother and my choice."

"Please don't come home with a mixed boy, it's bad enough your sister is a lesbian. And you, you have definitely done enough, I don't need you causing any more shame. Where did I go wrong with you two?" "Oh my God, goodbye mother." I didn't give her a chance to reply I slammed the red button and threw my phone onto my bed. The tears were gushing before I hit the pillow.

I heard my phone ring and ring and finally, I felt around for it, it wasn't my mom it was Rawk. The second I heard his voice I started crying all over again. "What's wrong who made you cry?" I was so embarrassed that those few words were all it took for me to unload but at the same time, I really wanted to tell him.

I gave him a breakdown of my lecture and heard his car pulling up outside Cossack House not long after. "I'm here Amarelia, open your door." He asked before disconnecting our conversation. I threw my door back and jumped into his open arms. "I'm sorry I caused trouble, I told you I was trouble you didn't need." "No I'm sorry I'm acting like an emotional wreck, it's my mother and it's been a long day!" "Yeah, it has how about we just crash? I REALLY need to sleep and not dream so kick me if I talk or anything but I'm exhausted. I think you'll sleep better too?" He tied up his hair and turned to me.

"Sounds perfect." I led him to my couch like it was the most natural thing. That's how I ended up sleeping with him for the first time, literally.

He mumbled a bit in his sleep but nothing crazy. His fingers were around my waist when I woke up the next day but other than that we were perfectly decent and God I felt so much better!

PRESSURIZED

I didn't see much of him the following
morning, which was good. It gave me a chance
to sort myself out for the trip to the convention.

We caught the train up (two trains and a ferry
actually) and were both out of breath and irate
by the time we arrived at the hotel. It was miles
from the station. We were wet and miserable
and colder than I think I've ever been in my
life. Rawk wanted to bring his car but there
was no way we would have gotten through all
this in the Triumph.

The only good thing was the further away from
London we got the calmer Rawk got. We had
the night off and agreed that we were desperate
for a hot meal. A local cabbie suggested a little
pub on the other side of town and when we
read the menu both of us grinned madly.

"God bless him." "Absolutely, oh my goodness
I want one of everything!" My eyes scanned
the card again. "So get one of everything."
Rawk shrugged. "Yeah, I don't think Callen is
going to pay for my lux supper night." I
laughed behind my menu card but Rawk
moved it down and waited for me to look at
him,

"Amarelia, order everything, fuck it order two
of everything, I'll pay for it. You deserve it
after those horrid train rides, it's the least I can
do, you didn't complain once and it's only
money." He shrugged. "Alright, Roccafella." I
teased

"I'm not the money bags that would be my father." He sniggered "So are your family rich or wealthy?" I asked straight out. "Very very rich, they are too fucked up to be wealthy though." "What's the difference to you?" I asked and his mouth curved at the corners.

RAWK'S POV

That question has always annoyed the fuck out of me because no one askes it correctly. No one asks for my version or opinion. She did though and without even having to think about it.

"You can have all the cash in the bank and all the houses and cars and it all means shit if there's no one to share it with. That's what makes you wealthy, the trust. That's the filling that holds the stuff up. A Partner, a family and genuine friends. I want a life and a legacy to be proud of and lots and lots of kids to love." She was the first person I have actually said it to beside Carys.

The thought of Carys poured ice water over me and my whole mood dropped. Amarelia, ever the observant one, must have noticed because she kept the conversation light for the rest of our time there.

When we left the drizzle had cleared but the pressure was building. I could feel it around me as well as within. What the hell was I doing with this woman? I was such a fuck up and somehow she knew how to handle me but it didn't change the fact that if anything happened between us my family would destroy her and from the little bits I knew of her family I was not their idea of a son-in-law at all.

We got back to the hotel and she made a beeline for the bathroom. Moments later I heard the shower and had to keep my dirty mind from swimming laps in the gutter. When the trips itinerary came through before we left I saw that we had been booked into a room with two single cots instead of two single rooms but selfishly I hadn't mentioned it.

I wanted to get to know her away from school, see if the person I saw daily was the real woman or if she just put on a truly good show. By the time we checked in, there was nothing that could be done about the rooms and she didn't kick-off. We spoke about the following day's plans and settled into our beds.

We were in separate singles but they were pushed together so I could watch her sleeping in the moonlight. It was so fucking unfair that I was so damn attracted to her, everything about her appealed to me. There was fuck all I could do about it though. University policy says no and my fucked up family would kill our relationship eventually if I didn't first. FUCK!

The following two days we dragged ourselves from lecture to unveiling and back again. At some point between the rose meridian and the Knights Templar, it had started snowing steadily.

We didn't dare venture out for fear of freezing and chose instead to spend the night on our hotel room floor playing board games. Rawk let his guard slip every so often then he'd catch himself and retreat back into his head. I wished I could tell him to just chill the hell out.

I was in the bathroom brushing my teeth the next morning when my mobile rang and Rawk picked it up. *"Sucki Aki's* calling, who is that?" He called to me "Shit my sister, just hang on." I garble trying to brush as quickly as possible.

"Hello." I heard Rawk say and soon my sister's voice came through the speaker sounding supremely confused. Oh my shit he was talking to my sister! "Er hi, I must have the wrong number." "No you don't, Amarelia says you're her sister."

"Amarelia says huh...yes I am and who are you, her boyfriend?" "No, I wish I'm her research partner." He teased me with a wink. "Oh too bad Lia could do with a good shag." "Oh my God Akia what the fuck is wrong with you?" I seethed at the phone making Rawk laugh aloud.

"Damn your research partner sounds gorgeous, is he?" "Yeah, he is." There was no point denying it. I cringed when he shot me a heated look. "Oh my God, *are* you shagging him?" "What Jesus Aki no I'm not shagging him." I blushed excessively and both Akia and Rawk bellowed with laughter.

"What's up, how are your visitors?" "Oh my God, I wish they would leave already. Mom is so angry with auntie Soula and what the hell did you do?" I knew exactly why my mother hadn't told my sister and the most horrible part of me itched to share but I wasn't up for the blowback.

"They were going to let me walk back to Uni alone so Rawk came to fetch me and he drives a Triumph and he has tattoo's and he didn't get out of the car to introduce himself." "And I'm mixed, don't forget that." Rawk said over my shoulder and Aki roared

"Oh, my fuck Ami wami I am so proud of you! A tattooed, mixed-race boy with attitude? Finally a real man! Now can you shag him so you can put that wanker behind you for good!" "The wanker is old history I'm long over him. Nothing has happened between Rawk and me yet, chill."

"Yet?" My sister asked. "No, I didn't mean it like that." I shot my eyes at Rawk and his brows rose with his smile. I should have turned speakerphone off long ago. "Yeah okay whatever little sis. I love you and I miss you and I wish you were here instead of the drama lamas." I heard my mother's voice getting louder and said the last goodbye.

NIGHTMARES

"Yet?" Rawk grinned "I didn't mean it as a presumption." I defended but he held up his palms to me. "No complaints. Who is the wanker?" "Oh um he is a long tangled story. Very summarised version, we dated but he lied BIG lies. He made my life hell both mentally and physically and is a large part of the reason I ended up coming to England, besides loving Callen's work." I looked up into Rawk's eyes and saw rage simmer behind them.

"He hurt you, like put hands on you?" "Right at the end, when things went pear-shaped we got into our worst argument and he chocked me. I fought back so hard that I broke two fingers before I passed out." It was so much easier to talk about it now, 18 months later.

Rawk was appalled I could see it and that old familiar shame washed over me. My mind automatically went back to my mother asking me what I did to provoke Josef when she arrived at the hospital. This straight after being told that I had sustained two broken fingers, a cracked wrist, four fractured ribs and multiple tears and bruises to my throat and jaw. Who asks what an eight and a half stone girl did to deserve that, whose mother asks that? Had I deserved it?

"Hey what's going on in that head?" "It's fucked up but a small part of me has always wondered if I did something to deserve-" "No, no don't even attempt to finish that sentence Amarelia. There is no world in which any woman deserves to be hurt. At all or ever, what he did was wrong." His fingertips grazed my jaw and he cupped my face.

"Why the fuck would anyone need to overpower you, you're so...little." He pulled me into a quick hug "He lied about his degree and I found out. I threatened to go to the police if he didn't resign from the practice." I mumbled into his chest. "Law?"

"Doctor, Paediatrics actually, and I couldn't allow it. Knowing that I really want kids, and if it were my child, I just I couldn't." I stepped back from him and shook my head as my eyes misted over.

"Hey no I agree with you, 100% yeah. You are amazing, what a wanker." Rawk ran his thumbs under my eyes and frowned deeply. He stepped away and said we should get a move on. The snow had really come down overnight and I seriously hoped our train was still scheduled to leave.

We made our way to the station slowly and our hopes began to sink as we were met with a terminal of desperate-looking travellers. The station master came out from a little office and was crowded in seconds. Soon Rawk walked back over shaking his head.

"What does he say, what's happened?" "You called it, no schedule until further notice." "What does that mean?" "It means we're stuck here for another night." "Shit and we can't get back to our hotel because the pass would have snowed over."

"Yeah, I think we're stuck here here until the weather clears. We should try to find somewhere to stay, the guy says it's the worst snowstorm they've had in a while." "Shall we try asking at that internet café?" I pointed. "Yeah come on then."

As we walked up to the counter, an opera of rather descriptive language rose up around us. "Storm's knocked out the internet connection, sorry people." The owner raked his hands through his already dishevelled hair. Mobile phones popped out almost as one.

"Landline has gone." A woman called from an office and looks of horror and resigned realisation stared back at us as we looked around. "Does anyone have a network on any platform Facebook, Twitter, Insta anything?" Someone asked.

Everyone tried desperately to get something but the truth was we were stuck and momentarily cut off from the world. "Now what?" "Fuck! Guess we have to go into that fucking storm and find somewhere to stay." "Okay." I zipped up my jacket and readjusted my backpack.

When I looked up he was grinning at me. "What?" "No hissy fit about going into the cold, I'm impressed." "Yeah well it won't improve the mood and I really don't fancy sleeping on the station floor," I admitted looking at all the lost souls loitering around.

We stepped out into shin-high snow and I wondered if we may still end up having to sleep on the station floor. Rawk pulled his beanie low over his ears and pointed at a dingy-looking nearby hotel.

That one, as well as the following two we trekked to, were all booked out. I was certain I had frostbite by the time we came across a sign that read *'The eyes of God see all things.'* Rawk and I grimaced but beggars couldn't be choosers. He stuck out his hand and I took it as we went up the steps.

"I guess they assumed we were a couple?" I tried to make myself sound calm when I looked at Rawk. His eyes went wide before he swallowed. "Actually...they think we're married." A nervous chuckle left him. "What?" I felt my cheeks heat.

"The owner's wife said she wouldn't allow any *youngsters* wanting to live in sin under her roof. She asked what my wife's name was and I just went with it, I'm sorry."

"Don't be silly it was absolutely the right thing to do, I couldn't face going into the snow again." He looked like he was about to stay something else but turned and made a fuss of unpacking what he needed from his bags.

"I'll take the couch." Rawk offered. "Are you sure only if you don't mind? You can share with me if it's uncomfortable." I blushed deeply and threw myself at the bathroom door. Only when I was fairly certain that Rawk would have settled in for the evening did I creep out and dive between the sheets.

"Goodnight Amarelia." His words were a low rumble that made me smile. "Sweet dreams." I was so exhausted I was out in seconds but it didn't last long. Rawk's tossing and turning woke me and I drifted in and out depending on how loud his whimpers got.

He started mumbling and thrashing and when his moans turned into loud talking, panic flooded me. I tiptoed over and tried to shake him. I called his name repeatedly and leaned in closer. He woke with a startle and pulled me down and onto him as he shot up.

I landed in his lap and froze. His eyes were wild and filled with tears. He ran fingers over every part of my face then exhaled loudly. Tears released and he folded forward into me. His big arms closed around my body and he pulled me flush against him. "I'm so sorry." He whispered and my heart sank, what and who the hell was he dreaming about?

Slowly he questioned his sight and I saw reality hit his face; I wasn't the girl from his nightmare. His eyes shot into mine and his arms snapped apart from me. I shook my head and gave him a sincere smile. "It's okay, you're okay Rawk. You had a crazy nightmare."

"Fucking hell I haven't had that dream in a long while, I'm sorry are you okay did I hurt you?" "No not at all you were starting to really panic and it made me panic," I said clearly and calmly but little strings of adrenalin still coursed through my body, I've never witnessed a nightmare so intense. I still shook slightly.

"It's the cold and the snow brings back bad memories." "Let's just share the bed okay? That way I can just kick you if you have another nightmare." I joked and he sent me a small smile "Yeah good idea, neither of us is going to sleep otherwise."

PLAY PRETEND

It *was* warmer with Rawk beside me even if he had rolled himself in the blanket like a burrito. I lay awake for ages though unable to settle. I kept going back to Rawk's nightmare making shivers streak across my body.

I've never witnessed such overwhelming fear. Whatever and whomever he dreamt of I wasn't certain I wanted to know. The pain in his eyes was terrifying. I felt my cheeks warm as the phantom touches of his fingertips swept across them.

I was still trembling at random. I had to calm the hell down. "You okay?" he rumbled beside me "Yeah fine why?" My heart slammed against my ribs. "You're shivering." "Oh no, I'm okay sorry." "Don't apologise, it's okay to be cold, here." He sat up and gave me another blanket

"Better?" "Yeah, thanks." It was better but it smelt like him and that was a different kind of torture altogether. "There is a better way to stay warm you know." He tested in barely more than a whisper. I was so weirdly turned on and freaked out by the entire situation that I called his bluff.

"Show me." I turned on my side and faced him, fluttering my lashes innocently. His smirk had a dangerous edge to it but the moonlight gave me courage. I could see him but I remained in patchy shadow.

Rawk snaked his hand under the sheets and around my waist. He tugged me hard against him until all that separated us was a single sheet. I swear I stopped breathing for a few seconds when he grazed his teeth up the shell of my ear, "If we don't stop calling each other's bluff you're going to end up getting in trouble."

"Why do you assume that you're the only one who is the trouble?" "You're too sweet to be trouble Amarelia." His fingertips ran along my jaw and neck. They skimmed my shoulder and floated down my arm. "You catch more flies with honey than vinegar, Rawk," I whispered against his lips and shifted my body up along his.

His reaction was instant against my hip. "Fuck! You are a dangerous, dangerous woman. Good night Amarelia." He moved apart from me and onto his back. He stuffed his blankets back around him and shot his eyes toward the ceiling. I grinned to myself, I win! "Sweet dreams." I purred seductively and he chuckled.

I woke up slowly and it took a few blinks to work out what was different. Rawk and I were no longer two separate burritos. Instead, we had joined and formed a croissant. He had as much of me covered with his body as humanly possible, I was practically underneath him.

My heart drummed furiously and I knew that he was awake when he sucked in a breath and ripped himself away from me as if I were electric. "I'm sorry."

"For what, obviously we got cold at some point in our sleep, it's okay Rawk." I turned to face him, making more space between us. He still looked shocked but stretched out. "I don't think I've slept for that long in years."

"Yeah, I gather you're not a peaceful sleeper." "I haven't been since I was a teenager." "Then I'm glad you slept well." "Yeah me too." He said but looked so confused by it.

We were on our way down to breakfast when Rawk stopped me. "What?" I turned into him and giggled an apology. He spoke softly and kept his hand around my waist, "You're meant to be my wife." His eyes bored into mine. "Excuse me?" "We're meant to be married according to them remember."

"Oh oh yeah, right yeah." I fumbled and thankfully he steamed on. "You aren't wearing a ring. Why would I not give you a ring?" "We could be all new age and not wear rings, I don't know?" I shrugged. In all honesty, I could barely think, Rawk saying I was supposed to be his wife had given me major feels! Shit!

He embraced me to pull the ring off his pinkie then slid it onto my finger. "Marry me?" He asked with THE most devilish look on his face. "Why not?" I smiled up at him and back down at my hand with his ring now on it. "What about you?" I asked quickly and he unclipped a chain from around his neck to let a ring fall off it.

"Right here wifey." He tapped my nose. "That's Mrs Amarelia North to you," I smirked and he whistled low. "Very dangerous words...Mrs Amarelia North, you will be the end of me woman." He ran his eyes over me before shaking his head. I giggled all the way into breakfast.

We exchanged looks all through the meal. There were some pretty strange people holed up at the B&B. Between us we kept the conversation going in a team attempt to avoid the attention turning on us, it was inevitable though,

"Tell us how you young lovebirds met then?" "She tried to kill me." "He nearly knocked me down." We answered at the same time and it was perfect, the table erupted with laughter. I let Rawk tell his version but interrupted to inject the truth. We laughed and blushed appropriately and by the end of breakfast, we had an entire romance going.

From our accidental meeting to the present day. When they asked about our wedding I paled and reflexively reached for Rawk's hand. He took it without question and I squeezed hard. Talk of marriage reminded me of Joseph and not in a good way.

His jaw clenched but he lifted my hand, kissed my fingers and smiled at the table. "It was a really intimate affair but I've promised

Amarelia's family a huge party during summer break." "What about your family dear?"

"My mother passed a few years back and I am sadly no longer close with my father." His big hand tightened around mine and I knew it was an avenue he didn't want to go down either. "But my family are so loud and many and we all love him very much."

I slid my eyes into his stunned face and blushed profusely. The corners of his mouth pinched and I could feel the relief rolling off him. He leaned over and pressed a kiss to my temple. It was such a simple intimate gesture and it made my heart stutter.

Coos and sighs surrounded us. "This is how the young should be living. You find your heart's match as you two obviously have and you forge a life together. None of the uncertainty and messing about rubbish." Everyone nodded as one and the look on Rawk's face was priceless.

"You were AMAZING!" I whisper shouted as soon as we shut our room door. "That was insane; it felt like we were on trial." His fingers raked through his hair repeatedly. "I think we were, partly." I flopped onto the bed and closed my eyes.

"So what would you like to do on the dead side of town during a snow in?" He asked sarcastically forcing me to roll my eyes at him. "It doesn't look that windy, how about we get out of this place for a while?" I didn't know how great an idea it was for us to be alone in a glorified bedroom all day. Rawk looked massively confused for a few seconds before replying.

WORDS & WHISKEY

RAWK'S POV

We pulled out our warmest gear and after suggestions from the other guests headed out. I didn't want to go too far in the shite weather; it wasn't worth the risk of Amarelia getting hurt or us getting stuck outside.

We made our way to the town square and into the little shops that were open then we found an old church to gawk at. I felt like an alternate version of myself out here with Amarelia. Sleeping with her was quickly becoming addictive. She was soporific and I found myself craving her affect...and her.

We were walking down the stairs outside the church when I slipped on a patch of ice. Amarelia reached out for me and caught my arm going down but I took her with me. She was knocked into the short wall and I bounced against her before landing on my arse. We wobbled back to our room slowly and I was grateful that we made it undetected.

"Christ my back hurts! Help me get my shirt off, yeah, I can't." I couldn't wiggle out of it. I tugged it up then she peeled it off my arms "Ouch!" She ran her fingertips up my arm making my eyes close automatically. "It would have been worse if you hadn't caught me, thank you, but also you shouldn't have done that. Did you get hurt?" This was exactly what

I didn't want to happen. "I'm fine." She replied and turned to her backpack.

After pulling out a mini first aid kit she handed me some painkillers then turned to pour a glass of water. Without warning, she folded over onto her side. "Oh shit, that is aw aw aw." She shuffled to the bed and dropped down onto her opposite side.

When I sat down beside her I noticed a layer of sweat now covered her face. "Where does it hurt, baby?" WTF? 'Baby' came out on its own steam and shocked the shit out of me, I had nothing to do with the decision but luckily she didn't notice.

"My side, it's breath taking." "I'm going to take your top off to see if there's any bruising okay?" "Yeah okay, oh my God how did I not feel that before?" "Adrenalin and you were all tightly packed from your jacket; it was when you took it off and started moving about." I ran my fingers over the already darkening marks across her ribs and down to her hip. God her skin was like silk. What the hell was I doing? I stepped back and offered the painkillers she had given me.

"I think you may need these more than me." "How the hell did this come from that?" "You went into that wall remember?" "Yeah, but I was so well insulated." "I weigh at least double what you do and you were going against gravity. It's a lot for such a fine frame. I hope nothing's broken." I felt sick at the

possibility. When I looked at her she was grinning and my eyebrows knitted together.

"Fine frame hey?" she fluttered her eyelashes and I shook my head at her. "I meant because you're small but yeah it is a fine frame too." I teased her and she flushed red. Jesus, I wanted to see that as many more times as possible. Shit...

"Let me feel your ribs yeah, tell me if there's a sharp pain." I hoped she knew the difference. "Yeah okay." She answered easily and I ran my fingers across her rib cage.

"There's no pain it's more of a dull ache. I think it's just bruised. Huh, I've never so much as twisted my ankle." She said proudly and I honestly had to bite my cheeks to stop the grin on my face, fuck! "I hope you're right." "You didn't do anything to cause me pain, this was all me besides now we have an excuse to have a drink?" Her eyebrows wiggled at me.

"I really shouldn't drink but I guess I'm cut off from the world and I can't get into much trouble around here so fuck it, yeah I'll go get us alcohol. See you soon yeah oh I'll get snacks too." I was babbling and I knew it. I needed air.

Her voice curled around me as I reached the door and halted me in my tracks.

"Hey Rawk you're wrong you know; you could get into a world of trouble just between these four walls." When I looked back at her she

winked and I knew I had to leave immediately.
I was in so much trouble but I was only just
realising the depth.

I laughed to myself; the look on his face was
priceless. I was glad to have time to freshen up
after he practically ran out. The thought of
what could happen did fill me with many
different feelings. I was part terrified and part
turned on by him and his temperamental
moods. I couldn't afford to fall for another guy
who would break my heart either way and from
the time I've spent with Rawk, I was pretty
certain that if he broke me I would stay broken.

He stormed back in a half an hour later and
huffed under his breath. "You okay?" "Yeah
fine." He spat out "Whoa okay." I took a bottle
of whiskey from him and turned toward the
desk. I watched him in the mirror.

"I'm sorry. When I got into town I got a
message come through from my aunt because
my father is sick and my family 'suggest' I
come home ASAP." He threw up his arms and
exaggerated his parenthesis. "You don't want
to see him at all?" I asked.

 "Are you gonna lecture me because if you are,
just save it." "No, no judgement or lectures
from me, I have no right." I got out quickly in a
bid to keep him calm. "Oh, I thought you might
give me the *'you can't say sorry when he's*
dead' bullshit." "Well you can't but that's

beside the point I think more importantly you actually have to be sorry in the first place and you obviously aren't."

"I can't fucking stand him." Rawk watched me closely as he said it. I think he was gauging my reaction. I simply nodded and handed him a glass of whiskey. Here goes nothing or everything.

"Would you like to talk about it?" "NO." He roared. "Okay!" I held my palms up. "It's just how come he gets to practically cut me off from and out of the family but now that he needs to clear his conscience I am good enough to be summonsed home. Why the fuck do I owe him anything? Because he's my father, well he was a shite fucking father and an utter bastard of a husband."

"You could use the visit to get everything out and maybe tell him your version of whatever happened?" I ventured carefully. "I can't believe that you still don't know, no-one has told you?" "Oh they've offercd but it's not their story to tell. I have stories I'd prefer to tell you myself because I know how twisted they would get if you heard them elsewhere."

"Would you like me to tell you?" "That's such an unfair question." I whined, "I know." He tilted his head to the side. "Yes I would like to know your truth," I confessed. "There now, isn't so bad admitting that your curious is it?" "I could say the same thing to you," I mumbled but he heard me. His finger slid under my chin and pulled up. "You really should filter what comes out of that smart mouth more it's gonna get you in trouble and I've already told you I am not the kind of trouble you need."

I poked the tip of my tongue out and ran it across my bottom lip. Rawk's eyes followed its path. He swallowed as he stepped back then gulped down his whiskey in one mouthful. Damn, did I affect him like that? "Dangerous Amarelia. Oh my God, even your name sounds dangerous, Amarelia Wolfe. Fuck I need to stay the fuck away from you, you'll undo everything." He mumbled more to himself than me.

CARYS

He started pacing and the entire mood shifted. "Rawk!" I called across the room. "What?" His eyes seized mine and he stood motionless. "I'm sorry, no more teasing and maybe we should skip the alcohol too?"

"Fuck! No don't apologize to me I should be apologizing to you." "What?" He was so damn confusing! "Pour us each one last drink; It's time to tell you my story." He stalked over to the bed and sat on its edge.

I poured then sat alongside him. "I've been driving since I was 14, on my family's farm and around town on backstreets. Not just cars and bikes but big things too like tractors and harvesters, I'm a good driver yeah." He stopped suddenly and took a big gulp of his whiskey. I smiled encouragingly and he continued,

"Carys was my first real relationship and a week after I got my learners license I took her out to celebrate. I know I know anyway, we got into a very heated argument over me beating the crap out of Damon Coleman. He was a senior at the time and a cruel dick who liked to pick on people. He also loved to push his luck with Carys yeah. Always throwing an arm around her because he knew it fucking pissed me right off." His fist clenched and he took a minute to calm himself.

"I just had enough; I didn't stop until I put him in the hospital." "Why was she angry?" "Carys is the only girl I gave the time of day to after my mother or had a relationship with and I believed I was in love with her but she didn't understand. She felt that me beating Damon meant I didn't trust her and she was humiliated." His eyes glazed and I reached for the whiskey to refill our cups.

I had a hundred questions but I was petrified to ask a single one. Where is Carys now, did Rawk still love her or miss her? He swallowed half his refill in one and carried on. "There was a patch of black ice and I oversteered. We ended up in the gorge trapped in the car. Our phones had rolled out of reach and it was one of the coldest nights of the year." My stomach dropped at his words.

"I held what I could of her all night trying to keep her warm, she had thumped her head hard and kept slipping in and out of consciousness. We were found the following morning under the snow." He threw me a tense grin then snorted.

"One of my dad's *people*, Jack Finch, is a cop and made sure the incident recorded had a licenced driver in the car with us so I got off from the law but not from my father. I have never been so scared in my life Amarelia. I thought we were going to die, she was going to die and it would be my fault." "I'm so sorry that happened to you." I squeezed his arm but he shook his head.

"When she finally woke up she couldn't remember anything after leaving the restaurant and I never reminded her. But it ate at me yeah, we started picking and arguing and I did the stupidest things. I started drinking and partying heavily, I was a fucking right mess. My ma wasn't around to set me straight and everyone else was too afraid of my temper. Jesus, I fucked myself up proper after that night." He rumbled as I ran my fingers across his forearm. His eyes closed and he sighed heavily,

"She transferred to London to our Uni and it was better for a bit in the beginning but my father was on my back about taking over the family business and us getting married. He was angry at me for wasting time at university."
"You two were going to get married?"

"Oh, Carys and I were a sure thing according to everyone but us. Mostly we were great but I had changed and so had she. She wanted a man and I was a broken boy." "So you guys broke up?" I asked quietly and he shook his head, tears rolled silently down his cheeks and he wiped at them roughly.

"Nah, we um we got into a massive row last year. We were in such a bad place by that point. She found me blind drunk on vodka at a sorority party with girls all over me. We had a huge argument in front of everyone.

She got high and started grinding up against a guy I knew had always liked her. All my years of fury drained into that scene. I don't think even I was prepared for the way I flipped out; I'm still ashamed of my behaviour that night." He lifted my fingers from his arm and held them to his chest before continuing his story. I thought my hand would sizzle off at any minute.

"I saw red and I lost my shit in an absolute fucking rage. I beat the guy she was dancing with unconscious and I put two of his friends in the hospital in a bad way. I fucking wrecked the house. I threw glasses and chairs and aggressively pushed and shoved countless drunken students around. Carys pulled me into her car before the cops arrived. I was so over the line that I carried on fighting with her. She took an old short cut to get us away from the party but she skipped the red traffic light."

His voice choked at the end and I realised why Rawk is the way he is. "She died?" I felt his sadness wash over me, he looked 10 years older in an instant. "On impact, I had a couple of broken bones and only avoided jail time because the CCTV placed us there at the time and her driving. The guys I beat up were too afraid to press charges but there was still an investigation, led by Finch. They would have chucked me out and stripped me of all my credit."

"You got a second chance." I offered "Yeah but I'm not sure how much of it has to do with my father so I haven't felt that I deserve it once." He sniggered bitterly making me knot my eyebrows together at him. "So then make yourself deserving, honour Carys, do yourself proud." "My family hate me and so do hers, they all blame me."

"That's because you blame you and you know what FUCK 'em." "What? " "Yeah fuck them, if their love is conditional than so can yours be. If you would like to see your father then you should go see him. If you don't and you can live with what that means then don't." "It's not that simple for me Amarelia." "But it really is Rawk. What do you need, not them, *you*?" I kept my voice low; I wasn't sure where my boundaries were with this.

"I don't have a fucking clue." The words came out in a long heave and he buried his head in his hands before raking them through his hair. "Hey, no one has to make any decisions right now. Want me to go down and see what's in the kitchen?"

"To be honest all I want to do is eat the rubbish I got earlier and drink till I pass out yeah." "Okay." "Okay?" "Yes Rawk okay, if it's what you need right now then why not, let's get trashed." I smiled widely and handed him another refill.

We were thoroughly drunk and on our final round of slapsies. My painful ribs had been anaesthetized by alcohol and I was giddy as hell. My legs ached from crouching on the bed. Our arms hung rigid and our eyes wide. The second I moved my hand he registered and I knew it was over.

He pulled back and countered with a stinging shot straight to the finger. "Motherfucker!" I cursed at my 'wedding ring'. They kept smacking together and I was certain we would both have bruised fingers.

"It's the ring." He slurred. "Sure blame the ring Mr happy slaps." I went to take the ring off but Rawk caught my hand in his. "Don't take it off." He slid it back up my finger and I had to remind myself to breath. "Um okay."

"Don't break the spell." He frowned as if he didn't understand it himself. "Huh?" "You, your spell. Whatever you've done, I haven't been able to casually have a couple of drinks or to sleep through a night in...Jesus...in a fucking long time. We get stuck in the middle of nowhere and I manage to have the best time I have had in ages. So don't break your spell, not yet yeah." I nodded mutely in response.

I lost the power of coherent thought for few seconds then the weight of his words set in and I felt overwhelmingly sad for the broken boy before me. I stepped into him and wrapped my hands around his neck then pulled him down into a tight hug. His body tensed but as soon as I felt his fingers wrap around my waist and squeeze I knew we were good He relaxed into me and sighed deeply. We passed out soon after that.

The following morning we received notification that the train station was up and running. We could head back to civilisation. To say that I was disappointed would be a fat old understatement.

TRAINS TO RAINS

I hated the idea, I liked this version of Rawk and I wasn't ready to give it up just yet. In its place I'd get university Rawk back. I think he felt the same while we packed up to leave. "Do me a favour when we get back yeah?" "Sure what do you need?"

"When I start acting like a dick again please PLEASE know that it's not you. It is never going to be you, I'm really fucked up Amarelia and you're really sweet and genuine and I don't fucking know how you do it...put up with me I mean. My point is when I do fuck up please remember this me, the me that you make me, okay." "Yeah okay." I breathed out while my brain tried to restart. His words had caused my mind to shut off for a few seconds.

We were sent off with travel snacks and the hungover me was supremely grateful. Our journey back felt like a last attempt to hold onto magic. We got off the ferry in Wales and continued onto England. Rawk had me practically on his lap almost the whole way back as we simply watched the landscape shape and mould, it was very lulling.

We jerked awake at the same time hours later and I smiled to myself. My legs were draped over his lap and my head was against his chest. My fingers had gone out on their own and found their way under Rawks shirt. As I slid them back I felt him chuckle. "Your fingers have a mind of their own when you sleep."

"Yeah the traitorous bastards are getting chopped off as soon as I can find replacements." I wiggled my hand in front of us and he laughed properly. It was instantly my favourite sound. "Do you think I'll regret not going to see my father if he dies?" He glanced up then immediately back down.

I slid my fingers down his forearm and curled my hand into his. "Maybe not immediately or even in a few years but eventually you will. Not for him but for you because you would have allowed him to make you a monster. His actions have caused your reaction but people will always assume you didn't want to see your family or dying father."

"Fuck, you're right! How are you so fucking smart?" He pulled my head toward him and planted a kiss on my forehead before snapping me back. I blushed at the sweetness of it. His hands dropped as he sighed. One found its way around my waist and the other rounded my kneecap. The sensation was beyond distracting.

"I don't know if I can do it though. An entire weekend is a long two days." He sounded so exhausted by the whole saga. "Don't you have some-one you could take along? It may be less crap if you have a friend in your corner?" "If I don't want to subject myself to that circus why would I do it to anyone else?" His eyes searched mine desperately.

"That's what the people who have your back are meant to do for you Rawk, have your back. I'm sorry your shitty father didn't show you that, he should meet my shitty mother they'd get along famously." I stood up and went to the loo. I needed to put some distance between him and I for a bit. I was starting to think stupid thoughts about us.

I swear I had to stop myself from offering to go with him. The only thing that stopped me was the possibility that I could have read this entire trip wrong. What the hell was I doing, I had to rein myself the hell in!

RAWK'S POV

We arrived back on Uni grounds to miserable steady rain and it was bone cold. That type of cold that bites into your muscles and throws darts at your face. My room was closer to the open parking lot and I didn't care who I had to explain to about why she stayed with me, Amarelia was staying with me, end of story.

I watched her remove her jacket and leave her umbrella outside before stepping into my room. I was so grateful I'd cleaned up before I left. "You have two beds?" She asked. "I am meant to have a roommate but no one wants to be stuck with me I guess. So that bed is now my research layout area." I tried to sound funny but it was more sad than cute.

"Well I am very grateful to be stuck here with you. I am looking so forward to a hot shower and a good old power nap." She beamed up at me and my head swirled. Wow! "Need me to scrub your back?" I teased. She clicked her tongue and huffed quietly. "Oh if only you

95

could." She joked except it didn't sound like she was joking. Didn't feel like it neither.

Was it possible that she was serious about her feelings for me? I admit I have feelings for her, I'm not an idiot. The woman gives me feeling feelings and it's scary as hell...and it's fucking me up. Wait what did she mean 'if only I could'? Why couldn't I? I mean I know why I shouldn't but she was saying it like...like what?

I had to know, I knocked on the door to my little en suite. She couldn't hear me and I was being ridiculous I turned away from the door but then the shower stopped. I walked back over to the door and listened for a few seconds.

The extractor fan buzzed to life and I jumped back but there was nowhere to go so when she opened the door she walked right into me. She put her hands out to steady herself. The towel that had been wrapped around her chest was now around her ankles and in its place was the flimsiest lace bra I have ever seen.

"Oh my God Rawk I am so sorry I forgot my top I was just coming to um sorry I just TOP." She yanked the t-shirt off the bed and slid it on quickly before turning around with red cheeks. Fuck she is just so out of my fucking league. "Nice bra." "Why thank you." She answered sarcastically but her grin told me she was okay with the teasing.

"Nice boobs too." "Oh come on you saw them for like a second, how do you know?" "So show me again, for a fair judgement I mean." I

frowned at her and she giggled her infectious laugh at me. She reached behind her back and after a couple of manoeuvres slid her bra out from her sleeve. I raised my eyebrows and she shrugged.

"What? I had that bra on the whole way here I just want to be comfortable now. You may have it since it fascinates you so." She mocked me. She had no fucking idea what she was doing to me, all I could think of now was the fact that her breasts were bare under that thin piece of fabric.

We hung out, like really just sat around laughed, talked and ate. It was incredible and I was so freaked out by it that I was even considering going to see my dad. I wondered if she would come with me, I was so tempted to ask her.

I wasn't joking when I told Siobhan that Amarelia is my person, in the past few months she's become the person who knows me best. But that was also the reason I didn't want to ask her. I didn't want to expose her to them and their fucked-up ways. The most selfish part of me didn't want her to know where I come from or what I came from, I was embarrassed to be a North and the heir to his empire.

ARRANGEMENTS

RAWK'S POV

*The rain never gave up for longer than a few minutes at a time and we both ended up in my bed because the only working radiator in my dorm room ran alongside its wall and it was cold **AF**!! Amarelia was telling me the unedited version of when Josef's mother and hers met up to arrange their marriage.*

"You're taking the piss, no way would that have passed legally." I narrowed my eyes at her but she held a finger up. "Slow down big man, they would have found a way to trust me. Thankfully my father found out and threatened to leave her if she so much as tried to arrange me in marriage to anyone I hadn't chosen for myself." "Shit seriously?" "Yeah, and in our culture, that is like beyond shame."

"You couldn't have been too popular after that?" "Oh I've never been popular, my brother was meant to be me and I was never supposed to happen." "What?" "My mother got drunk one night with aunt Soula and they got into a fight because she said something along those lines, I heard it all but when I confronted her about it she said I was making things up and Soula separated us before I could say anymore."

"And things have just gotten worse since?" "Well yeah because then everything came out

and Josef tried to kill me. She told me, and I quote, I am a worse shame to her than Akia and she's a lesbian." "Fuckin hell!" "Yeah tell me about it. Leila, the girl my sister shares her life with is the most amazing human and makes Aki so happy but our mother just can't fully accept it."

"Is that why you said I couldn't wash your back?" Finally, I asked the question that had been in the back of my mind the whole time.

"Yeah because...agh you know what I'm just going to be honest with you. I'm starting to develop feelings for you and I don't know what to do with them. My concern is that if anything serious happens between us I'll fall for you and then if it fucks up it'll really fuck post-grad and me up. Plus you're white and mixed so you're like a double no and I'm not even taking your tattoos or past into consideration" She shot me a burning gaze than looked down at her hands again.

"Does any of that bother you?" I clenched my fists waiting for her to answer. "Not even one little bit." She shook her head immediately. "So define serious then." "Sex." I couldn't help but grin and she laughed beside me. "So if we don't have sex we aren't serious?" I moved my finger between us. "What are you getting at?" She turned to face me and my eyes went straight to her lips.

"I want to kiss you and not just a little peck on the head yeah, I want to kiss you kiss you." I bent forward and our lips were a breath apart.

"So kiss me." I didn't give her a second to say anymore, my lips smashed into hers and when she whimpered it sent me into nerve ending overdrive. "God you feel amazing." I ran my hands up her arms and wrapped them around the back of her neck.

She felt so small and delicate under my fingers and it made rage flick through me like a bolt. I couldn't believe what that dickhead had done to her or how her mother had reacted. I would never let another person hurt her; she would be safe by my side for as long as I could keep her. SHIT! I pulled apart from her without warning and she froze.

"I'm sorry, did I do something wrong?" She asked when I tensed and released my jaw. My heart melted for her. "No baby you did nothing wrong. How about that nap?" I stroked her cheek before pulling her into me and shuffling us down onto my pillows.

There was nothing I wanted to do more than peel her clothes off and lose myself in her body but she was right; if it all went south I would break her. What she didn't realize is that she would obliterate me because even though I was trying not to, I knew that I had serious feelings for her already and they only grew the more time we spent together.

Rawk woke me up with coffee and I think I fell a little bit more. I took a huge gulp. "I'm going for a run; I know it's not your thing so you just stay." "Actually I really need to go back to mine and sort through some stuff. Give me 5 to change?" I practically sucked the rest of the coffee down in one go. "Yeah sure." I could tell from his tone that he didn't believe me when I said 5 minutes.

I changed back into my now dry clothes and threw my hair up in a knotted mess. I grabbed my bags and was at the door in less than 5 minutes. "Impressive." He smirked. "Nah I'm lazy with nowhere to go." I joked back. He tied his hair back before stepping up to me.

"Do you have to go?" His finger trailed up and down the back of my arm. "Um, why?" I checked absently. "I like having you around." He shot me an uncertain grin and I couldn't stop my smile. "Why don't you come and get me after you've had your run and done your bits? We could go have bacon rolls, fresh off the grill?" I offered and he bit his lip before nodding. "Sounds delicious."

"How the fuck do they make them taste like this?" Rawk closed his eyes and savoured his food. I giggled alongside him. "They fry the bacon in clarified butter and the buns are made on site." I stated. "Amazing." He purred. "Yeah, they are amazing." "Not them, although they are fantastic, you are what's amazing." He leaned over and kissed my nose. It was the final crack to my defences; my Rawk walls were officially crumbling at all points.

We drove back in companionable silence most of the way. It was a flawless winter's morning.

"What would you like to do with me Amarelia, where shall we go?" Rawk asked innocently enough but I heard the double meaning in his wording. "I would like to go to Starbucks with you, get a take-home order and then go back to yours and have dessert." I played coy but he didn't laugh. I sighed internally.

"How about we agree to stay in our bubble for the rest of the holidays and when we get back to class we can see how we work out while trying not to get bust?" His head nodded but he looked saddened by my answer. I leaned over in my seat and dropped my head onto his shoulder. Here's to honesty;

"Rawk I'm fascinated by you and I imagine I would need at least a lifetime to get enough of you. I like all the sides of you, even the ones that scare me a little. If I'm honest what I want from you is the hope that we could work romantically because we would be so good for one another. I want you to say that you won't let go of me, but I have no right to make those demands of you yet." I shot him a quick glance.

His hand slid from the steering wheel and pulled mine onto his leg. "I could promise to try for you? I am really not the best person for you at all Amarelia I know that. My family is severely fucked up and so am I but I am also selfish enough to admit that I just want you. I like you way more than I have *honesty* liked any living thing in a long long time." All his anger and attitude was replaced with fear. I saw it in his eyes and on his face, this was unknown territory for him.

"Will you just try to trust me Rawk. If you can then we'll be fine, you will never have a reason to get angry with me. I'll always be honest with you but I need the same back." I stated and he caught my eyes in the rear view mirror, holding them for a few seconds before looking back to the road. "Okay." He answered and I swallowed deeply. What had I just signed up for?

We ran back into his just as the rain was starting up again. "You may have to spend the night if this is only the beginning of it." Rawk told me as he unlocked his door and took a bag back from me. We spread out our sugar coma buffet and warmed up our coffee in his little microwave. I loved being with Rawk for this reason alone, we could truly just chill.

Our afternoon was spent watching *'Ancient Aliens'* and working our way through all our junk food. At some point, we must have dozed off. "Amarelia let's go to bed yeah, it's fucking cold." Rawk prodded me in the side and I stumbled around the couch toward the bathroom.

I came out with one eye still closed and ready to drop onto his bed but he tossed something at me. "You are not putting that sticky top in my bed." He teased and I giggled quietly but agreed. I was a mess. "Maybe if you hadn't waffle slapped me I wouldn't be sticky." It was dark enough that I quickly slipped my top off and Rawk's one on. I decided to keep my leggings on even though I knew I'd have a rash in the morning.

JUST FRIENDS

RAWK'S POV

She had no way of knowing that the window behind her gave her body a perfect silhouette in its light, fuck she was sexy! She slipped in beside me and I had to restrain myself from pulling her against my body. God, she smelt like sugary sweet heaven.

*"Goodnight Amarelia." I murmured and felt her shiver. I loved that I could get that reaction out of her. "Sweet dreams." She replied in a gravelly whisper and I felt my cock twitch against my boxers. Christ! This internal war had to end. I knew I shouldn't want her but fuck it I **really really** did.*

Something was wedged into my back and it woke me. I looked over at the radio clock, 3:33 in the morning. That was a fair amount of sleep for me. As I turned she purred my name and it shot blood straight to my groin. Suddenly I didn't care about sleep. I lay opposite her and studied the face that had stolen the broken bits of me and started gluing them back together.

She has the most perfect lips, fuck she is perfect full stop, fuck! Fuck fuck fuck!!! Was I really capable of doing this with her? The thought terrified me slightly, so much could go wrong.

She makes me feel everything when all I want is to keep knowing nothing.

She shifted onto her back exposing her shoulder to me and I had to mentally slap my own hands. I wanted to run my tongue along her skin, she looked so soft. God, what was happening to me? I raked my fingers through my tangled hair roughly.

"I want you, I don't care." She groaned and I knew she was dreaming, but of whom? I watched her dream play out, it was never anything more than a murmur or a mumble. Soon I began to doze off then she said my name again. I perked up and paid attention. "Yes, I'll marry you." She slurred and I frowned deeply WTF? "I love you." She sighed before moaning and I had to wake her before I did something to fuck things up.

She opened her eyes and smiled widely at me as she focused. "I had a dream about you, you asked me to marry you." She giggled quietly and I felt my brain pop and crackle. Absolutely no filter on this girl. She said she loved me in her dream. I decided to play it cool, "What was your answer?" "Yes obviously." She grinned and I knew there and then, she was mine. I wanted to claim her. Fuck my family, her family and the faculty.

"Remember how you said that it was only serious if it was sex?" Here goes nothing. "Yeah?" She narrowed her eyes at me. "So does that mean we can do other things?" She came up on one elbow and I thought my head

was going to explode. Her hair was a wild mess and my shirt hung off her body, exposing her collarbone and breast. It was my undoing.

"Other things like what?" She asked taking me completely by surprise. "Like touching every inch of your skin, like trailing kisses across your ribs and down your spine." "Fuck stop speaking Rawk. You have no idea how difficult you're making this, we're meant to be figuring things out." "That's rich, you just told me you dreamt I asked you to marry me." "It was a dream, that's not fair." She shot at me.

"Yeah, sure whatever but I dunno if I'm capable of 'just friends' with you." I pummelled my pillows and pulled the blanket up. I knew I was overreacting but I couldn't help myself. I was so confused by my feelings. She shook her head and turned away from me but I had most of the blankets so she was forced to shuffle closer eventually.

She wiggled her arse inches in front of my dick and it responded immediately, Jesus buddy! "Fucking hell what are you doing Amarelia?" "Sorry, it's my leggings they had to come off, all done." She lay back in position and her words sank in. "So that means you don't have pants on?" I whistled low and because I simply couldn't resist I ran a fingertip up her thigh. Fuck it was so smooth.

"Umm yeah, but I have your shirt on." "Oh baby that only makes it sexier," I whispered in her ear as I pushed against her. Shit, she felt incredible and fit into my body like she was

made for me. I slid my hand across her stomach and up between her breasts. It went around her neck and I felt her gasp. "What are we doing here Rawk?" "Whatever we're allowed to but I can't be just friends with you Amarelia. I wouldn't do the things I want to do with you to a friend."

She rolled her hips against me and my cock slipped between her cheeks. It nestled between the two globes and she began to slowly move up and down. "Fuck me!" My hand went back down her body and dipped between her legs. She was slick and ready for me when I slid a finger into her. "Oh God, you are so wet for me." She moaned in response and I felt her small fingers wrap around my cock.

"I don't want to be just friends with you either Rawk but if we do this you have to try and not let go or run away or shut down on me." Her hand stilled around my shaft and she turned to look at me. "Here with you right now, there's nowhere else I've ever wanted to be more. I'm trying to be good enough for you baby, whatever you want me to do I'll do." My words were the truth and they must have convinced her because she turned fully in my arms and gazed up at me with her bedroom eyes.

"I want you to put your cock in my mouth." She licked her lips slowly and I thought I'd shoot my shot right there. She dipped her head and kissed her way down my stomach. I gripped the sheets tight around my hands

"Good morning Mrs North." Rawk tapped his ring to the one I still wore and I smiled so deeply that my cheeks ached. "Sleep well, husband?" I blushed when my eyes met his. Sure we hadn't had actual sex but damn it we had done everything just short of it. I felt the bed drop as he sat.

"Thinking naughty thoughts wifey?" He ran his lips around the shell of my ear and whispered the words. I swear I felt my insides liquefy. "What if I am?" I called his bluff. He cocked an eyebrow at me and chuckled "Then it would be my duty as your husband to fulfil your needs, so what do you need?" He was going to push as far as he could. Well fine, I'd just push back. "You." I purred and the little gasp he made was so satisfying.

"Rawk, you in there? It's Nicky, have you seen Lia? Rawk, RAWK!" Nicole whined from behind the door and both of us burst out laughing, typical! Rawk got up and bounced over to the door, throwing it open to a shocked Nicole. "Fuckin hell I can hear you, so can half of London. Come in yeah." She walked in and I watched her face trying to decide which expression it should wear when I sat up in Rawk's bed, in his t-shirt.

GOING NORTH

"OH MY GOD!" Her eyes swung wildly between Rawk and I. "Calm your tits it's not what it looks like Nicole." I started. "Yeah, we got back from the field assignment yesterday. I didn't want her to be alone in the storm so she's stayed here." Rawk clarified and I was so grateful for how unfazed he sounded.

"So you two aren't shagging?" "NO!" We both roared and she shrank back. "Fuck me okay sorry I had to ask." "Why do you have to ask?" I questioned and the room went absolutely silent for a few seconds. Nicole and Rawk were looking at one another weirdly. "What?" I flapped my arms. "Tell her Nicky she knows everything else."

Rawk came to share the headboard with me and Nicole leaned against the desk opposite us. "So Rawk's told you about Carys and the accident and fighting etc?" She asked and I nodded, not trusting my voice.

"Carys...she was sexually assaulted just before she transferred to London. Her drink was spiked at a block party and when she came around she was in a *Travelodge* room with used condoms all around her. She wasn't the only one. There were 2 other girls also." Nicole spoke rapidly.

"One of them was 15, the other barely 16. Carys had such a baby face and she never wore makeup so they probably thought she was around the same age." "They were purposefully looking for underage girls to drug and rape?" I asked and Rawk snorted beside me. "Well one of them definitely knew exactly who the girls were." He shot a filthy look at Nicole and her face softened. "Yeah I'm with you but there was never any hard proof, no one knows who the guys were." She answered quietly.

"Carys went off the deep end and when I finally got it out of her I demanded she goes to the cops. I spoke to the other girls and they agreed to go as well. Chloe remembered some of it. She recalled her rapist having a goofy tattoo on his wrist because he kept his hand over her mouth when she came around and started screaming." Rawk hissed. My eyes widened. "Coleman?"

"Damon was never caught because there was no evidence." Rawk spat out, so that was why he got so pissed off at the ball. "But you said there were condoms." "Yeah turns out the cops never recovered anything of the sort." "Oh my God! So he got away with it. No wonder you hate him."

"It never made sense to me that whole story, Chloe was adamant it was him. She even agreed to let officer Finch do a lie detector test." Nicole shook her head but my eyes flew up to Rawks. Could it be? "What about Vicky?" I asked and both shuffled awkwardly. "Vicky committed suicide." "On her own or with help?" I whispered to Rawk and his eyes bulged.

I didn't know what to say or where to look. So did that mean that Rawk's father knew about Carys and the others being raped? Oh my God, what kind of person was he? I understood why Rawk didn't want me to meet him. He was watching me with scared eyes and it tore at my heart. I squeezed his fingers in mine. "That was not your fault." "No, but if I wasn't being such a dick to her at the time it wouldn't have happened at all."

"Thank you for sharing with me but I don't understand how us potentially being together and those events could have anything to do with each other." Loud banging startled all of us and Rawk jumped at his door. He ripped it open and bark out a loud 'WHAT'. Stuart and Siobhan stood in the doorway. "Have you seen Nicky? We're going up to North Manor and she is supposed to be coming with." I heard Siobhan ask.

"Fuck sorry guys I totally lost track of time. I was trying to convince this one to come up. Do you have my bag Shivvy?" She rushed the door, blocking me from their view. "What are you doing here?" That came from Stuart and I didn't miss the undercurrent on his words. He was jealous. "She's not your girlfriend she can talk to whoever she wants." Rawk replied neutrally but I could imagine the look in his eyes.

"I'm well aware but there's hardly anyone on campus and it's not all that safe is it?" "Alright alright, whatever let's go. You should come up Rawk, He really does wanna see you. " Nicole squeezed his arm and left with a backward smile in my direction. He shut the door and locked it before leaning against it with a deep sigh.

"Hey only if YOU want to...I could go with if you want?" I offered carefully and watched so many emotions run over his face. "I truly don't want to go, I haven't even told you all of the stories yet but I also know that what you said is true. I need to go for me."

"You could go up for a day or two and stay in a hotel. You don't have to stay at his." He seemed to be considering it as he walked over and dropped down next to me. "Okay." "Okay?" I couldn't believe I'd convinced him. "Yeah okay but I can't leave you here alone." "Rawk I'll be fine I'm a big girl." "You're my girl and I don't want to leave you so...come with me?" I felt myself melt on the inside. He trusted me.

"Sure." I gave him my biggest smile. "God, you are something else. Okay let me call my aunt and we'll get going yeah?" "Okay but I have no clothes or anything. Could we go past mine on the way out?" He nodded and started speaking into his mobile. I did what I could with what I had in the little bag I'd brought back the previous day.

After stuffing what I needed into a backpack we left campus and started the long drive to Cardiff. I was looking forward to seeing St-brides-super-Ely, the town was meant to be incredibly scenic. Rawk told me the rest of his story as we drove.

By the time we hit Slough he had covered how his family made their money. His father now owned and ran *North enterprises*. It had been added onto and passed down for generations and he was meant to head it next.

By Reading, I knew that Rawk suspected his mother's death wasn't an accident and that his father had essentially cut him off when he vowed to find out the truth. He travelled to France often to visit his mother's family and they felt the same as he. He wanted me to join him the next time he went. I simply agreed, he had never been so forthcoming and I didn't want to ruin it.

Crossing the Prince of Wales bridge nerves set in. I had just told Rawk more about my relationship with Josef when he turned to me. "I don't want you to come with me when I see my father." "That's alright. I will wait at the hotel." "You don't mind. I know I dragged you here but I don't know what I'd do if he said something." "Hey it's fine, you should catch a cab that way I can come to get you if it gets really bad." I joked, well half-joked.

"You'd come to save me from my family?" He kept his eyes glued to the road and I was grateful for it. I slid my fingers down his forearm and wrapped them over his. "I've got your back Rawk, I'm your people remember?" "Yeah, yeah you are." He pulled my fingers to his lips and kissed them before sighing deeply.

Doubt curled up against my limbs like smoke,
what the hell was I doing?

*Only **EVERYTHING** I'd been told **not** to*!

MOST HATED

RAWK'S POV

You'd come to save me from my family?" I kept my eyes glued to the road. I couldn't bring myself to look at her while sounding so vulnerable. She slid her small hand along my forearm and placed her fingers over mine. "I got your back Rawk, I'm your people remember?" "Yeah, yeah you are." Pulling her fingers to my lips I wanted to tell her that she had become much much more than that but it wasn't the right time so I sighed deeply instead. I had to get this over with ASAP then I could go back to figuring us out.

We had just passed the Fairwater green when the cop car appeared in my rear view mirror. "Fuck sake!" "What, what's wrong?" The light flashed just once and I pulled over. My heart sank; that signal meant that the body walking toward my car could only belong to Jack Finch, fuck! I was so sure I would be able to hide Amarelia from my family that I hadn't even considered the rest of the town.

"Do I need to be a sleeping student catching a ride home for the holidays?" She offered as she covered herself with the blanket she had brought along. "I could kiss the fuck out of you right now," I whispered as my window slid down.

"Rawk, you alright or what? Thought that was you, coming to see the old man?" "Chief Finch, yeah aunt Sara called." "Good one your aunt. Saw Siobhan and Nicky come through earlier." He said in passing then shot his gaze to Amarelia

"Who's the merch bert?" He slid his eyes across her face and I wanted to bash his teeth into my door. "She's in Callen's class. She needed a ride here and he knew I was coming up. She's been asleep most of the ride." He seemed satisfied. "Good to see you Rawk, stay out of trouble." He patted his fist against my window and stepped back. As soon as he was back in his car I saw him pick up his two-way radio. Fuck!!!

"He's the chief now?" She stayed down and it made me want to swing my car around and go back to London. She shouldn't have to hide. I shouldn't have to hide her. Fuck this and fuck my father and if my family took sides then fuck them too. All I needed was beside me. "Yeah, he is, largely thanks to my family. Fuck I've got to do this once and for all. I'm going to see him and then I'm done. If my family don't want me then fuck them too."

She straightened up and smiled widely at me. "That's the spirit!" She cheered and I simply had to laugh out loud. I was in so deep with her. I prayed we made it out of here together. "Come here." I pulled her toward me and she snuggled in. "It's so beautiful here Rawk." The smile hadn't left her face and it made me actually look around.

"Yeah, I guess it is." I never paid attention anymore, it had become background. My father's background. "I would love to live in a town like this with a big plot of land and lots of kids and animals." Her eyes danced and my stomach dropped. "You'd be okay to live here?" "Are you kidding this place is lush." She giggled at her own use of the local term and a tiny balloon of an idea inflated in my head.

I booked us into one of the few places that didn't have a connection to my family and showed Amarelia around. We were away from the main town so I tried to relax and see my birthplace through her eyes. Eventually, the call I was dreading came through. He knew I was here and wanted me to come home.

"It's time, my Uber is here," I called to her in the bathroom. "Uber?" Her head popped out. "Not gonna lie your idea earlier was brilliant." I shook my keys at her and she grinned. "I got your back babe simply call me and I'm there." She teased taking the keys to my precious Triumph. I gave them willingly; **she** was most precious to me.

Driving into North Manor I tried to imagine what she would see. The rose-covered walls and the manicured gardens but all I saw was greed and lies and loss. This was a house built on the blood and bones of the dead. Generations of my family have lived here and they have all been wealthy. If you can call getting rich through exploitation wealth.

"Aunt Sara." I gave Siobhan's mother a tight squeeze and she cupped my face looking me up and down. "It's good to see you lad, good thing that you came." She turned me toward the stairs and led me up. "He's not been very well this morning and he may be resting now. Shivvy and Nicky were here earlier." I wondered where they'd stashed Stuart.

"I won't be long. I just have to get some stuff off my chest." Her eyes widened and I clenched her forearm gently. "There won't be any trouble from me I'm over all the fighting. I just wanna say my piece yeah." Her eyes searched mine then she patted my hand. "You're a good lad Rawk. I'm sorry things turned out as they have."

"Yeah me too," I replied, she didn't know the half of it. Taking the stairs to my old room two at a time I thought of the shit she must have put up with over the years. My aunt Sara was married to Colin Finch, owner of Finch financials and brother to Jack. He knocked her up with Siobhan while she was dating his best mate and rumours of affairs on both sides have always lurked. This is what I meant when I said my whole family situation was fucked up. Sara is the oldest of the 4 North kids and has always looked after my father, her baby brother. I got what I needed out from under the floorboards I had finessed years ago and made my way back.

I walked into my parent's bedroom and had to take a minute, the only good memories this house held for me were made in this room on the floor with my ma. I shook the ghosts away

*and walked toward the bed. I was shocked to
see how frail my father looked but I just
couldn't find it in myself to feel anything for
him. I sat heavily and only then did I notice my
uncle Barry in the corner watching me.*

*"Alright?" It was the first word I'd said to him
in more than a year. "See you finally decided
to come make peace." "Hmm, something like
that." I sniggered and Barry sat up straight.
His eyes snagged on the wedding band I wore.*

*"What the fuck happened Rawk? I tried
speaking to him but he wouldn't say a thing
only that you were cut off." "A lot of bad shit
has happened under his command. I just had
enough of it and threatened to expose him."
"Expose what?" My uncle pleaded and without
even trying I had my audience.*

*"Don't you think it's funny how shortly after
my ma threatened to leave him because of the
affairs and tell her family about his dodgy
business ventures she ended up dead?" "Jesus
lad that's your father you're accusing there."
"Then all that shit that went down with
Carys." "He had nothing to do with that
Rawk." "No? How certain are you?" "What
do you mean?"*

*"I'll tell you about the common thread between
all these events? The cop in charge of the case
and his fucked up but well-connected family.
Chief Finch kept me out of jail when I crashed
at my father's request. He was in charge of the
rape case **at my father's request.** "*

"He wanted to keep the press away Rawk, good God what kind of man do you take him for?" Barry was getting flustered and it made Sara come to the door. "And why did he want to keep the press away so bad? I'll tell you why not because of embarrassment or privacy but because Chloe knew that it was Damon who raped her."

"WHAT?" Sara hissed from the doorway. "I'm sorry aunt Sara but it's the truth. She drew the tattoo for me." "It could have been a coincidence." She was grasping. "Green jumper wonky ear, it was Damon. Then Vicky ended up dead and Chloe ended up getting sectioned didn't she. Judge Coleman threw the case out."

"She got sectioned because she lost her mind." "Yeah, after Jack let Damon see her and he told her that if she didn't shut up he'd be back to finish her off." "No, it can't be, oh my God. Have you told Emily?" "I haven't spoken to your sister since the day she married Damon's father. I have absolutely no reason to lie. I came here to clear the air and set the lies straight."

Beside me, my father stirred and coughed. "Rawk is that you?" "Yeah, you summons me so here I am." "Go get the others, Sara." He barked and she scurried out. "What's going on?" Barry asked. "I'm making a few changes to my will brother. I needed everyone here to witness it so that there isn't any bullshit after I'm gone." I rolled my eyes but bit my tongue.

If I could get through this quickly I could get back to Amarelia and we could go home.

Siobhan, Nicole and a few other family members gathered in the room than in walked Carys's cousin. I wore my shock on my face and he had the decency to look mortified. "Rhys, what are you doing here?" " He's joined his father's practice and is here to update my will." My father's voice was hoarse and he had to be helped up. Rhys placed all the papers out on the table and explained what would happen upon my father's death.

If he thought that saying I got nothing would affect me he was sadly mistaken. What he still didn't understand is that the money and stuff stopped meaning anything after my ma's death. I truly didn't care. After all the signing malarkey was done I stood before my father and breathed in deeply.

"I forgive you for everything you did or had a part in. I hope you find your peace and when your time comes that you can go with a clear conscience." "As if you won't be the first one trying to get your hands on everything. The only thing you will ever touch from North Enterprises is what you are connected to with that fucking farm. See this is why I cut him off." He told his audience. I snorted and shook my head. Suddenly he was strong again and pushed toward me until we were inches apart. I grinned when I realised that I had bulked up in the last year and was more than a head taller. He had to look up at me.

*"I don't want your money old man and I definitely don't want this land or house. You killed every bit of good about this place when you had my ma murdered." His fingers flew across my face as he turned beet red." Get the fuck out, you are dead to me. You hear me, **dead**!" He screamed into my face. I shook my head, Amarelia was right I needed to do this. "I was dead to you the minute you helped covered up Carys being raped by Damon and his gang of paedophiles." Aunt Emily gasped from the outskirts of the room. Rhys looked up sharply as I turned to leave.*

I could hear them all shouting but I didn't care. I had done what I came to do and now I could leave. "Rawk," Rhys called and I turned to him. He looked sick. " I only took the job because I wanted to find out the truth and I thought if I got closer I could find a clue or something."

"You don't need to explain to me and you don't need to associate with that family to find out the truth. I'll tell you the key to it all right now. Go back on the cases and find the common threads, find how they all tie together. You'll have your suspects." I squeezed his shoulder and turned. "There's a clause in the will. Well, I put the clause in because of your mum." "Say what now?"

"If you are actually married before your father dies you get everything that was once hers." "What?" "Yeah, I stumbled across it and added it to the update." He grinned innocently at me and I stood rooted to the spot in shock.

"My ma owns the farm." "Yeah, and she always wanted it to go to you and your children one day. Also, your father has been moving business into her name recently to evade taxes." "That would all become mine?" "Everything in her name." He confirmed with a grin. "Huh."

Suddenly an idea became a plan...

FOR REALSIES

It felt like Rawk had been gone forever when my phone sang beside me. "Hey, you okay?" "You were right. I should have done this ages ago." "Want me to come get you?" "Yeah I'm done here, let's go home baby." His words washed over me and I felt giddy from them. I had fallen for him, hook line and sinker. Hell if he asked me to give up my life and follow him to the South Pole I would. I left immediately.

"*Fuck me!*" I said out loud as I drove through the gates of North Manor. It was gorgeous and it was **huge**. Just how much money did his family have?

"Wow this place is quite something," I told him as he scooted me over so he could drive. "I wanna show you something better." He had a twinkle in his eye and I felt excitement bubble up between us.. "Okay."

We drove until we reached a farm. Like a proper sheep in the fields farm. "Oh, my goodness Rawk this is my dream." I sighed into his chest as he held me tight against him. "It was ma's pride and joy. Wanna come run it with me?" He asked quietly. "What?" "Turns out she left it to me, a little detail I was only just made aware of." "It's incredible."

"Is that a yes?" "Wait you're serious." I squeaked. "One hundred percent serious." "Would we still finish post-grad?" "Not what I was expecting you to ask. You can if you want but I would make this my life and give up

125

University as soon as I took ownership." He chuckled softly. "And you want me with you?" I checked. "I want you forever." "Forever?" I repeated the word. Holy shit on a stick! "Yeah I'm all in Amarelia. You told me not to let go...well this is me holding on. I'm done saying no to you."

"I'm in too." Fuck it I know I love him and I know he loves me, even if he hadn't told me in so many words. Nothing else really mattered. "Yeah?" "Yeah okay let's make this dream come true." I looked into his eyes and knew I was a goner. His smile was full and utterly gorgeous.

"You do realise that it means you'd have to marry me one day?" He said seriously and my heart started beating furiously I'm my ears. "Rawk I'll marry you the minute you ask." "You hardly know me yet." "Do you really believe that?" I deadpanned. "No in all honesty you know me better than any other person, alive or dead." "Exactly." I grinned triumphantly.

"Come on let's get out of here before someone sees us and calls the cops." He turned me toward his car and we walked back in silence. I was trying to wrap my head around what he had just asked and I was certain he was taking stock too.

Our drive to the hotel was quiet and we spent the night discussing whether we could realistically achieve the goal. I assured him that I was in and wanted to be with him but I also knew that if we both quit at the same time Callen would be down two researchers. At present, he was associated with only a small section of the farm but it was nowhere near to the time he'd need to devote to running it full time. Horticulture is a whole different level of farming.

"You'll stay until the end?" Rawk inquired the following morning. We went to a little pub for dinner and passed out shortly after. It felt beyond amazing to wake up next to him and as soon as he had ordered room service he picked up on our discussion.

"Only if I can't find a sub. If I can it would be sooner." "So we're really gonna do this yeah?" He asked from behind me. "How serious did you say you are again?" I joked over my shoulder but my eyes were lost in the view, the sight never got old.

RAWK'S POV

The moment couldn't be more perfect. I scratched in my jacket pocket then dropped to one knee. "Amarelia Wolfe with this ring I pledge my heart to you. All of me I want to share with only you as we build a life together. Take this ring as my commitment to marrying you when we're ready." Her eyes swam with tears but her smile took over her face. "Yes Rawk, yes to today yes to tomorrow and yes to marrying you. YES to all of it." She gushed as I slide my mother's ring on and it fit perfectly.

"How, when?" She looked at the ring then at me. "It was my mother's ring given to her by my French grandmother. It's a family heirloom and now it's yours until you give it to our daughter one day." The thought of Amarelia carrying my child sent blood rushing straight to my cock. She smirked at my crotch.

"You wanna put your baby in me Rawk?" She asked through her lashes and all my control shrivelled. I spread my hands around her waist and lifted her. She wrapped her legs around me and her gravelly laugh filled my ears, God I love that sound.

"Yeah I fuckin do, I love you woman and I want the world to know it yeah." "Then let's make our first child husband." She held up her finger with my mother's ring on and beamed. I looked down at my own hand, I didn't realise I still had mine on.

I grinned wickedly and walked us over to the bed. "What will your family say Amarelia?" "I know my mother will hate me but I don't care. I want you Rawk and I choose you and whoever doesn't like it can fuck right off." My mouth smashed into hers and we kissed like addicts who couldn't get enough.

I placed her on the bed and hooked her pyjamas pants with my thumbs. They came off in one swoop and the creamy skin that met me underneath had me groaning. She was so perfect; how the fuck did I get so lucky? I dropped to my knees and buried my head between her thighs.

She was soft and silky and I had to pace myself before I exploded everywhere. She pulled my head up and kissed me deeply. Knowing that she was tasting herself on my lips turned me on more than I thought possible. "My turn." She pushed me back and stood then pointed at the bed. "Lay down." She ordered and I dropped willingly.

"Jesus Amarelia I'm going to cum if you don't stop," I warned, she had my entire shaft in her mouth and was going up and down in slow lazy sucks. She let my cock out of her mouth with a pop then climbed on top of me. I lined myself up and she slid around me slowly. "Oh my fucking God you feel like heaven." She rounded her hips and slammed into me hard. It was my undoing. "Oh, baby, do that again." I moaned and she did it, slower this time.

I wanted her under me so I wrapped my hands around her waist and flipped us over. She giggled as I did and my heart hammered. I was in love with her, fucked forever in love. I just pray to God she didn't let go of our magic...of me.

DINNER PLANS

It was almost dusk and we were about to set off back to London when Rawk came barrelling into the room. He was sizzling at someone through his mobile and looked angrier than I'd seen him in a while. I sat quietly on the bed and watched him pace. His breathing became more laboured and every muscle in his arm tensed.

"NO!" He barked the one word out making me jump. He turned on me and I watched his face soften into a smile. His fingers tilted my chin up and he gave me a searing kiss before stepping back. "No Aunt Sara I don't want him anywhere near her and why do they care anyway?" I knitted my brows together and he gazed at me intensely before pulling his mobile away from his ear.

"My family are all here and are having dinner at North Manor. They want me there to clear the air since I am no longer cut off." His voice was flat and he looked so deflated, I couldn't tell how to read him. Did he want to go or not? "Would you like to go?" I asked tentatively. "I have to show up whether I want to or not. They want me to bring you with, that's what fucks me off." "How do they know I'm here with you?"

"My best guess would be Finch, am I right Aunt Sara?" He asked returning the phone to his ear. I took his disgusted snort as a yes. "Nosy old fuck!" Rawk clamped his jaw tight and breathed heavily. "If you want me to I'll

130

go if you don't I won't." I offered and he told his aunt he'd call her back.

"Baby I really don't want to take you to them but I can't leave you here. Finch probably knows you're here and I don't trust him one bit. Plus my father has definitely told him what I said." "Jesus Rawk you make them sound like the fucking mafia." "Close enough, actually I may have an idea." His fingers tapped his phone screen furiously then he was back to pacing, waiting for a reply.

"Champion! I don't wanna expose you to my family so I'm taking you to Nicky and Stuart. Siobhan will come to dinner with me. We'll try to be back as quick as possible." He ordered and I wanted to protest but I could almost feel the relief seeping out of him so I pressed my lips together and swallowed my words. "Okay." I gave him a big smile and he pulled me up into his arms.

"Thank you for not fighting me on this." He dipped his head and kissed me until my toes curled. "I just hope Stuart and Nicole don't hate me for interrupting their alone time." I cringed and Rawk pulled a face at my discomfort. "I am so sorry baby, I owe you one yeah." He teased and I had to admit that this Rawk was my favourite, calm Rawk. I also didn't hate his new need to call me *baby*.

We left and the drive was a short few roads away. Tucked away among the trees stood a series of little cottages. The sign over the gate read *'Forest getaways'* and Rawk shot me a wicked grin. "So many questions I'd like to ask. Seriously though Amarelia, if anything goes down or you start to feel like you need to get out call me. I programmed my number into your speed dial, just press 3."

"Why number three?" "I don't deserve number one yet and three is easier to find." His answer stunned me. "As soon as we leave I am making you number 1, idiot." I frowned deeply at him. His lips pulled into a gorgeous smile. "I love you Amarelia and I don't get why you want me but I am so fucking glad that you do yeah." "Yeah I really do," I replied. It wasn't poetry but it was Rawk and I loved him and all his crazy.

"So what were you guys planning on doing before I gate crashed?" I tried not to sound guilty. Stuart and Nicole shared a split second look before they both shrugged and shook their heads. "Probably just hang out, watch the tele or get drunk until Shivvy gets back?" Stuart offered but Nicole dismissed him with a hand in the air. "We could go down the pub?"

"No ways Nicky, Rawk was deadly serious when he said he would kill me if ANYTHING happens to Lia." He confessed and I was so grateful for Rawk's bad-boy image. "Great well what are we going to do then?" She huffed and flopped onto the couch. "We could have our own New Year's party?" I suggested. "Oh my God yes I love that, we could get all dressed up and everything." Nicole was already tugging me to her bedroom.

She wasn't joking when she said we were taking things seriously. Nicole zipped me into THE tightest dress I have ever worn and even more attention-grabbing was the fact that it was white. I'm not talking like nice purity virginal white no I mean skin-tight Lycra in NEON fucking-look-at-me white. Poor Stuart was going to go into cardiac arrest when he saw Nicole. Her dress was sheer net with very strategically placed diamante and just barely skimmed her thighs.

"Well damn darlin' you look good enough to eat." I heard Stuart whisper to Nicole and she giggled softly. Geez, what a fucked up situation? I didn't know the story though and it wasn't my business. I walked out loudly complaining about Siobhan's dress being too small for me when Stuart let out a low whistle. "Please leave that on for Rawk to see you in." "Why?" "Just trust me. It's something he will want to see. Or at least take a picture for him." He looked me up and down quickly then cleared his throat.

Nicole placed bottles of alcohol on the table and told Stuart to stop being a perv. We all laughed loudly at that and the earlier awkwardness seemed to lift. We had only just poured our second round of drinks when knocking had us all jumping up.

"Who's there?" Stuart asked loudly and immediately the knocking stopped. "Chief

Finch, we received a noise complaint. Please open the door, sir." He turned wide eyes on me and Rawk's words came creeping back. "Hide in the bathroom," Nicole told me and I did what she said without question. If I was totally honest I was more than a little freaked out that Finch had shown up to where Rawk had brought me.

"Must be a different cottage Chief, we are just having a quiet drink before we head out," Stuart answered Finch's question confidently. "You're not going to dinner at North Manor with Shivvy and Rawk?" I watched him ask Nicole directly and my blood ran cold. I heard Stuart's inhale and knew that something was very very wrong about this.

I pulled my phone out and pressed 3. "Who else is here?" Finch asked suddenly and there was a long silence. During that silence, Rawk picked up and the loud shouting in the background was amplified by my stupid phone speaker (I really had to fix that if I lived).

The bathroom door flew open and before I could move Finch appeared. "You! You're the girl from the car." I heard Rawk call my name. "Having a pee here. I go to University with them, what's it to you?" I tried sounding tough and failed miserably. "Better watch that smart mouth girly before you end up with my fingers in it." He leaned in and murmured into my ear. I felt revolt shiver up my spine and held back my stomach.

"Your little *merch bert* will be joining you shortly lad, I'll make certain to make her journey comfortable." He said into my phone and handed it back to me. He pointed at the door and I knew I had zero options but to do as told. Nicole and Stuart followed quietly and the ride over was completely different from the last time. It was dark and eerie with whipping winds whistling and licking past shadows. I couldn't wait to see Rawk, I was scared, really scared.

THE DRIVEWAY

We were marched into the house and immediately Siobhan appeared. She looked torn between running out the front door and blending back further into the crowd. There were enough people to be classified as a crowd and they currently all had eyes on the three of us. "Why are all of you standing around like mute donkeys?" Finch groaned, inching Stuart forward. "Well well, sticky Nicky haven't seen you in a while." A boy teased while looking her up and down.

I had the foresight to swap my mile-high heels for flats but poor Nicole looked ready to walk into a nightclub and I could see how uncomfortable she felt. I pulled my coat tighter around me and took a discreet step back. Before she could reply Rawk came tearing into the foyer.

"Fuck off away from Nicole Ian you know she can't stand you and for fuck sake stop with the *sticky* bullshit." He growled as he passed a teenage boy, flicking his ear hard. The kid bared a striking resemblance to Siobhan. Rawk's eyes searched and when they found mine I saw fear and relief staring back at me.

As soon as he stood before me I felt the tension leave my body, I was safe. "Baby, I'm so sorry I can't believe that my father is such a cunt." "When can we leave?" I whispered and Rawk took a step back. His eyes swept over me from top to bottom. "What happened, did he say something to you? What did he say?" Rawk watched me carefully and I didn't need to answer for him to know that he had guessed right. He narrowed his eyes at Finch.

"What did you say to her?" He was visibly shaking and I knew that things could take a serious turn. "Rawk just leave it. Let's just do this so we can go home." "Home huh THIS is his home girly." "This stopped being my home the day my mother was murdered." Rawk hissed and I didn't miss the gasps around me. Finch laughed the comment off as he strode into the dining room with a chuckle.

Siobhan took Nicole's hand and she took Stuart's as they shuffled behind the stragglers to take a seat. I looked up at Rawk and he shook his head before leaning into me, "Please don't take anything my family says seriously, especially my father. I will try to get us out of here as soon as I can." "Okay." It was all I could get out. I thought my family were bad.

"Who are these two?" An older, smaller and meaner looking version of Rawk asked when we sat. I could see the features he had gifted his son but Rawk was a beautiful lion compared to his rat-like father. Siobhan answered quickly "This is Stuart, Nicole's boyfriend and this is Lia she is at Uni with us." She answered shortly, keeping her eyes down and I felt Rawk squeeze my thigh when my eyebrows rose. "Nicky you finally found a man." Rawk's father stated before letting out a rattle of coughs. Sara offered him a glass of water and the entire table held their breaths.

RAWK'S POV

A part of me wished for a second that he would choke and then I knew I had to get out ASAP. Someone was going to say or do something that would make her leave me, myself included. "Please don't ask any questions until we leave, it's a long story." Siobhan dipped her head between us and murmured then smiled sadly at Amarelia. I really had hoped to avoid all of this completely. Fuck my father and Finch fucking Finch, I felt rage lick across my skin and clenched my fists tight.

Her small hand-fitted into mine and I couldn't stop myself from kissing her temple. The kiss was caught though and my uncle just couldn't help himself. "Found a replacement lad?" Nicole inhaled sharply and I didn't need to look to know that Amarelia's jaw was on the floor. "I am not Carys's replacement and why would you say such a cruel thing either way?" Her voice carried clearly over the stunned silence and Barry turned a deep shade of pink before my father interrupted.

"So my son has told you about his late fiancée." I felt her fingers pulse in mine but she never let her face slip. I was so fucking proud of her. "He's told me about a lot of things." She replied calmly and my father paled momentarily. "Well, I hope you're not with him for the family fortune. He did tell you that he inherits nothing if he isn't married before my death?" Of all the things he could

have said, this was the one that I thought may give her pause for thought. My promise has nothing to do with his will. She looked over at me for a few seconds before running her fingers through my hair. I felt my heart pick up pace, if she left me because of this I would kill him myself. "Guess we'll just have to move the wedding forward then my love." She purred seductively and the entire fucking room erupted around us.

"Jesus Christ you two are fucking made for each other." Siobhan shrieked as we burst through the front doors. We made a mass escape. "Did you see your father's face? Oh my God, I thought he was going to explode he was so angry." Nicole was high on adrenalin, her wild eyes proof of it. "My parents are going to shit all over me, fuck!" Siobhan lamented.

"You have got to be taking the piss!" Rawk nudged his cousin and her eyes zoned in on the lone figure walking up the drive. "Oh fuck me who invited him?" "Who is he?" I asked Nicole and she whispered her response into my ear, "That is the guy Siobhan is meant to be marrying. His name is Peter and he is an absolute fucking wanker!" My eyes shot up to Stuart and she shook her head. Things were starting to make more and less sense now.

"Peter what are you doing here? We were just leaving." He came forward to kiss Siobhan but she turned her head and his mouth made contact with her cheek instead. He smelt like he'd swum in aftershave. "Your uncle said you were here for a few days, he said I should come over so we can catch up, I have something to discuss with you anyway." Siobhan turned toward Rawk and I and her face was a picture of pure panic.

"Actually we need to leave now. There's been a change of plan." Rawk bit the words out and it didn't take a genius to work out that they did not get along. "Why would Shivvy go anywhere with you?" He sneered back and before anyone could stop them they jumped at one another. I had seen fights from afar before but to hear the sound of Peter's nose breaking made me feel sick to my stomach.

Within seconds the human content of the house was stood around us. Siobhan and Stuart had separated the two bleeding ragers but it was obvious that Peter needed his nose fixed and the split across Rawk's eyebrow was pumping out enough blood to suggest stitches.

"Rawk we need to get to a hospital." I held his chin gently in my hand and watched the gash ooze. "Go, we'll catch up just get him out of here before someone says something else and he really loses his shit," Nicole suggested and Siobhan was quick to agree. Rawk had used up all his adrenalin and didn't argue when I pointed toward his Triumph. "Is that the best you got?" Peter shouted. I turned and levelled him with a look of pure loathing.

"Enough!" I held eye contact until he looked away then unlocked the car door. Peter tried to rush us but Siobhan stepped in his way. "She said enough." "Yeah and who the fuck is she anyway?" "She is the ONLY reason my cousin isn't spilling you all over the fucking drive now please just fuck off Peter, we're leaving." Siobhan nodded at Nicole and Stuart and they turned toward their car.

"You can't leave we need to talk about the plans." He grabbed her arm roughly but she shook him off. Rawk tried to sidestep me. He wanted to go back for more. "There is no deal arsehole, there is no us and there will never be an *us* so forget about any plans, Peter." The rest of the North family moved closer. "Go, Lia, the shit's about to hit the fan and Rawk will kill him," Nicole warned me. I tugged Rawk back and shoved him into the car.

AN ABSOLUTE WANKER

I followed Rawk's directions and made him sit while I got the forms to fill out. Slumping next to him, I started filling out information but Rawk sniggered and stood. I watched in confusion as he walked to the little desk and handed back the clipboard. When the woman behind the counter looked up I heard her gulp before picking up a telephone. "Could you send nurse Emma down Rawk North is here and he needs stitches." She dropped the receiver and apologised. "Maureen it's alright please don't apologise I just need a few stitches and I'll disappear."

A woman came through the doors and immediately huffed at Rawk. "Fookin 'el I told ya ta stay outta troubles didn't I. Who did this ta ya?" "Hey Em, I got into an argument with Peter." "Ah gotcha, is the wanka still 'oping to score Shivvy?" "Something like that, can you fix me?" "Course I can, how'd ya get 'ere?" He turned to me and held his hand out. I stood beside him and the woman smiled widely. "This is Amarelia and this is Emma." Rawk introduced us before we went into a little room.

While she prepared all the bits she would need she told Rawk local news but kept stealing glances at me. Rawk hadn't let go of me since I took his hand. "Who woulda fought Pe'er would know how ta frow a punch huh." She teased as she threaded the needle. She had the strangest accent but I loved it, it was warm and comforting. "You alright hun, not gonna pass out on me?" Emma asked once she was ready to start. "I'm okay." I tried to make my voice even but on the inside, I was shitting myself. Rawk pulled me closer before Emma started. "Don't let go yeah." "Never." He squeezed my hand hard as the needle dipped into his skin.

"All dun wif ya, you alright?" "Yeah thanks, Em, can I go now?" He asked and I shook my head slightly when she looked at me. "Yeah you sort yourself out we'll catch up." She told him and led me out by my elbow. "What's he not telling me?" "I think he hurt his wrist but he won't say because he wants to leave, could you just check it if you don't mind and I'll take him to a hospital in London if need be?" She smiled at me "You're a good girl, yeah I'll 'ave a look. Wanna wait out front in case he kicks off?" "Yes please," I admitted with a blush and scurried along.

I had only just sat down when Sara and Finch appeared. I groaned internally and hoped that they wouldn't notice me. No chance! Finch shot me a grin that made my skin crawl. "Is Rawk okay?" His aunt asked nervously. "Yeah he is, Emma is just looking him over then we'll head home." "You should stay over. It's not safe to drive at night." She suggested but I shook my head. "I'll take my chances thanks. I think it may do Rawk more damage than good if he stays here."

"What's a pretty little thing like you doing with that lad anyways?" Finch sat opposite me and I automatically pulled my arms tighter around myself. "The only problem with Rawk is his family. They don't give a shit about him and

cast him aside when he needed them the most."
I shot back. "Oh you think so and who do you
think kept him out of jail?" Finch bent forward.
"Yeah, and why did you have to follow orders
to keep him out of jail? Maybe because you
knew that if his queries got to the right ears
they would have serious repercussions. Sara's
eyes darted between us. He laughed out loud.
"Oh, that's hilarious." The conversation
stopped when Emma walked up to us.

"Chief, Sara how are ya?" Emma barely made
eye contact before turning to me. "Rawk's
asking fa Mrs North." She said to me before
turning away with a nod to the others. "His ma
is long gone. Peter must have landed a good
shot to that lad's brain." "Peter's lucky Rawk
got pulled off him when he did," I said as I
stood. "Where are you going?" Sara asked me
but Emma answered her. "I said Rawk is
asking fir her didn't I. I've always loved the
ring. His ma would be so 'appy." I looked back
at Sara's dropped jaw and Finch had gone a
strange greenish-grey colour.

"Thank you for saving me!" I exhaled deeply.
"Ya was doing alright on yer own. So glad
Rawk's fallen fir someone wif a mouf who'll
'ave his back." I smiled at her words. "Always,
he's my people," I told her and she tapped my
arm before saying goodbye. I thanked her
again and went in.

"Hey, you." I ventured, uncertain of what
mood he'd be in. His eyes found mine and he
walked me into his arms. "I'm sorry baby."
"For what? You did nothing wrong, you were

standing up for Siobhan. It's all over now, let's go home okay." I seriously hoped we could bypass the waiting room. He let out a deep sigh and pulled my chin up before kissing me.

"So it's true then, you two are in a real relationship?" Sara stood at the door watching us, she looked almost scared. "She's my everything Aunt Sara. I'm sorry about the drama but I'm not sorry about Peter. He's a dickhead and he will treat Siobhan like shite. I can't believe her father wants her to marry that absolute wanker." He couldn't keep the disgust out of his voice. She shook her head and tears pooled in her eyes. "I'm going to speak to Colin, I didn't want to believe what she said but I saw it for myself tonight." "That's good, stop the cycle of unwanted marriages yeah."

We walked out to the waiting room. Finch seemed to have disappeared but when we got out the main door he was stood there with Barry and Peter. "You fucking tosser you broke my nose," Peter mumbled from behind a wad of tissues. "Lucky that's all I broke yeah." Rawk answered back as we passed them. I glared at him and tugged Rawk along.

I didn't hear Peter but Rawk did. "What the fuck did you just say?" He spun around and my heart sank. "I said tell that stuck up girlfriend of yours to stop giving me looks." "Yeah that's what I thought." Rawk laughed out loud and I heard Barry curse under his breath. "Rawk leave it," Sara begged and to his credit, he carried on walking with me.

Peter must have thought Rawk was scared because Finch was there so he got braver. "That's right fuck off back to school with your foreign bitch. Let the men look after the business." He shouted behind us and I felt Rawk stiffen. He looked at me and against everything I knew was right I let go of his hand. He snapped forward and kissed me hard then took four giant steps toward Peter.

"You can say what you want about me, I couldn't care less but don't even for a fucking second think you'll get away with saying shit about my girl yeah." His voice was a very low rumble. Peter was stupid enough to laugh in his face "The great Rawk North oohhh I'm so scared. Fuck you and fuck her."

A loud crack resounded around us and when I looked for Peter he was on the tar, down for the count. Rawk shook out his bandaged fist and stood over him. "Absolute fucking wanker, this is the scum you want your daughter to have children with? Jesus, I am so done with this family and its bullshit. Let's go home Amarelia." He told his aunt then held his hand out to me.

LAWYER UP

RAWK'S POV

She slid into the car and I catapulted us through the open gates. The adrenalin and rage that had been pumping through me ran out and incredible pain burnt through me in its place. My hand felt like it had been crushed in a vice. I swear she could read my mind because not minutes later her hand ran along my forearm. "Are you okay, I can drive if you want?" She asked carefully and my heart burst. I did not deserve her! "Yeah, my hand's fucking sore thanks."

I pulled over and we swopped but instead of taking off she turned to face me. I raised my eyebrows and after a slight hesitation, she looked me dead on. "I know that you giving me this ring has nothing to do with your father's will." I didn't know that I needed her to say it aloud but she did. "Fuck I love you, I will never deserve you but I am crazy in love with you." I pulled her fingers to my lips and kissed them repeatedly.

She slid her hands along my jaw and gave me the softest kiss. "I thought that if there was anything that could get you to leave it would be that," I confessed honestly. "I love you Rawk and if marrying you sooner rather than later means you get what your mum wanted you to have I would do it gladly. Just the same as you said this ring is you holding on to me, accepting it is me saying I am never letting go of you." She smiled up at me and my vision blurred. I wiped at my face roughly and pulled her against me.

"I don't think we will make it to London tonight." Amarelia sighed. "Yeah give me a second I think I know where Siobhan and the others might have gone." I was still tapping at my screen when hers rang. She asked me to see who it was but the number was private and for some reason it made my blood boil.

"WHO IS THIS?" I roared into the phone. "Jesus calm the fuck down, its Nicky." "Where's your phone?" "Rhys said we shouldn't use our phones after staying at North Manor. That's why I'm calling you on Lia's." "Yeah that actually makes sense, wait why is Rhys with you, where are the others?" I was so beyond over this whole situation and I could feel that old familiar dry rage sizzling through my body. The line crackled and voices muffled before Rhys started talking.

"Rawk I need you to come and meet us. I have something really really important to discuss and it concerns all of us." "Right now, it can't wait?" "No...um, in fact, we should have had this conversation months ago when I started piecing all this shit together," Rhys confessed quietly and I swallowed hard.

"Where are you?" "Remember where we fetched Carys and Chloe from after they thought they'd try ballet." An involuntary laugh escaped and I shook my head. "I

remember, see you soon and Rhys - good call on the phone yeah." "Be careful Rawk. Use the service parking around back." I dropped Amarelia's phone onto my lap and caught her concern filled eyes in the mirror for a second.

"Change of plans baby. We have to go to meet Rhys and others. Is that okay?" I rubbed her knuckles back and forth, the sensation calming my anger. "Sure, where to?" No questions and no arguing, dear God I loved her. I kissed her cheek and felt her smile against my lips. I prayed this all worked out, I couldn't lose her.

We pulled into a small motel and Rawk directed me around the back. A big sign pointed to staff parking and after making sure his car was hidden we made our way toward the strip of rooms. Nicole and Stuart were smoking and bickering at the entrance to the stairs and led us up to the room in silence.

"Alright Rhys, what the fuck was so important that it couldn't wait?" Rawk asked as soon as the door shut behind us. "Sit down Rawk," Siobhan suggested. "Why?" "It's about your ma and...all the other stuff." His legs seemed to buckle at the mention of his mother. He planted himself in a chair and pulled me onto his lap. Siobhan's eyebrows shot up but before she could make a comment Rawk turned to Rhys. "What's going on?"

Rhys handed him a thick pile of papers. "All the proof I have gathered on my cousin and

Chloe's rape, Vicky's suicide and your mum's murder." Rawk's head shot up. "I started looking into things as soon as I qualified and could gain access to the files. Your comment the other day threaded some of my pieces together. People know the family connections so no one ever questioned me." He answered my unasked question.

"I thought you did wills and estates?" Rawk asked. "Oh I do, I'm a qualified notary but I did a double major, the other is criminal law. I'm also legally ordained and have a black belt." "So what are you doing with all this?" He pointed at the papers.

"That's where you come in. I was wondering if you'd like to help me bring the whole sick lot of them to justice." Rhys murmured. "How?" "I need you to visit your grandparents in France." "We can do that but why?" Rhys's eyes darted between mine and Rawks and he asked to have a private word between them. I didn't like it, my stomach sank, something was wrong.

RAWK'S POV

Rhys shook his head and led me to the little balcony. He slid the glass door closed and turned "She can't go with." "WHAT?" I think I growled, actually, I'm pretty sure I made some sort of growling sound at Rhys. The poor guy pumped his arms out in front of me. "As soon as your dad gets even a sniff of what's going on, who do you think he is going to send Finch after first? If she's not with you she can be somewhere no one knows. Finch only has so much reach and I'm guessing she's not from here with that accent. Ask her to go home or on holiday, trust me there is so much more to the story Rawk. Lie to her if you must."

"You're right and I absolutely agree but I don't know if she will agree. I don't think I can lie to her and she will put up a fight." I don't want to tell her to let go...I don't want to let go of her. I thought she'd be the safest right beside me. "You love her so don't involve her. She loves you, she'll wait." The words streamed out of Rhys and I had to say I was impressed.

My head told my heart to calm the fuck down and play the scenarios out. "I'll talk to her when we head back to London yeah. It's going to be a long drive." "I'm sorry man I know it sucks but you know they will be watching us none stop."

Rhys slid the glass door open and Amarelia stood on the other side of it. When she looked up our eyes met and I knew that I wouldn't lie to her, I didn't want her to go. She crossed over and slid the door shut. "Hi, thank you for inviting me to the VIP lounge." She giggled at the silliness of the tiny balcony and I pulled her into my arms.

Her eyes found mine and her body tightened against me. "Did Rhys say that you had to get rid of me?" She sounded like she was joking around but I could see the dread in her eyes. "Yeah but here's why and here's what I think we should do about it, if you agree." "Okay."

She answered me softly and we had an intense conversation.

We went in and I gave Rhys a single nod before pointing Amarelia to our bedroom for the night. We never slept through. I told her everything, the whole truth. What I knew about my father and the Finchs. About Carys, Chloe and Damon Coleman. I didn't try to make myself sound better than I had been with all of it. I know I behaved like a twat and I own it all.

Also, she knew me, no matter how much we joked on it, Amarelia knew me better than any other person ever has. "So what are you going to do about all of this?" She asked me after I'd made my last point and I slid my fingers along her jaw, wishing all this was over already.

"I'll contact my grandparents in France. They have one of the best PIs in the world as a friend. I'm hoping he will help. Rhys actually has a pretty damn good case. He got Chloe out. She says she'll testify but I don't know how long that's gonna take and I'm not sure how safe it is for her to be about town." My eyes watched for her reactions. She smiled and turned her head to the side.

"And what shall I do all this while dear husband?" "Visit your family or what about your gran in the States, Aki you could see your sister." "Okay okay stop trying to sell it to me I understand. I don't like it at all but I understand. Before we go to bed I need to apologise to Rhys I was a bitch to him earlier."

"Hey Rhys, could I have a word." She called to him. He was still at the little table hunched over his papers. "What's up?" "I have a few questions and suggestions but mostly I owe you an apology, none of this is your fault and I snapped at you." "Oh um, I thank you that's wow okay." He looked so flustered, the poor guy. You don't get a heart like Amarelias very often. She gave him a minute to pull himself together and started to question him on some of the documents.

MCDONALDS

Breakfast was a quiet affair. We were huddled around a table at the 24 hour Mac's and it was 4 am. I had slept a total of 3 hours before Rawk nudged me awake. Rhys suggested we get out of Wales ASAP and Rawk agreed. I am not a huge fan of early mornings as a rule so I was extra quiet. "Hey, are you alright?" Rawk asked when we got back in his car. "Yeah, I'm fine, too early for me." I yawned for the millionth time and Rawk chuckled.

"What?" "Just wondering how you're going to cope on the farm. It's a pretty early start." I took his words in then grinned. "I'll be snuggling in bed with our babies Rawk, sorry but someone has to look after Sky and Pie." He laughed until he had tears in his eyes. "Oh my God, you were so drunk that night." "Excuse me I was tispy and FYI I would never name our kids Sky and Pie." "No, what would you name them then?" He smiled widely and I went with it.

"Hmmm, I like Selene and Sebastian." "So we're having a boy and a girl yeah?" "I mean that's if the first two are a boy and a girl." "The first two, how many babies are we having woman?" "As many as you can put in me." I laughed when his grip on the steering wheel tightened and he shifted in his seat.

"I swear Amarelia after this is sorted we are going to take over my ma's farm and I'm gonna love the shit out of you for the rest of our lives yeah." "I know" I stole a kiss and he pulled me into his side.

Connor lost his shit, he was furious when he found out we had left already. He blamed Rawk for everything and demanded that he come back to Wales or he would come to London. So we found ourselves back at a McDonald's desperately trying to piece together a plan. "You and I could go back up and speak to him. We could leave the girl's here?" Rhys offered.

"Nah first thing he'd do is send Finch after me," Chloe told him and we knew she was right. Ian called Siobhan earlier and said Connor was seething and had called a big meeting at North Manor. He said a few dodgy looking guys had dropped in already.

He didn't know Chloe was out but as soon as he did Finch would be up both of their asses. Rhys ran his fingers up and down Chloe's arm and she smiled at him. I couldn't even begin to imagine how she felt. Siobhan, Nicky and Stuart stayed at Uni, Nicky was trying to get hold of her aunt to send Chloe to.

We didn't want to draw attention and we needed a plan pronto. "What if I get David Whitehair to sub for me and I go visit Aki...and I take Chloe with, I mean if you want. Sorry I know we hardly know one another but I just want everyone to be safe." I grimaced but her eyes shone back at me. "You would do that for me?" She whispered. "Oh, Chloe of course I would. We may not know one another very well but I know what it's like to live in fear and I know that you mean a lot to Rhys. He's helped me so much already, so yeah I would love you to join me."

She smiled widely and brushed away a stay tear. "Thank you. Do I have to go to Rhys? I mean do I have the money for a ticket?" Rhys gripped her hand in his. "I know I just got you back but sending you away is necessary to keep you safe, you get that right?" "I do, I trust you. You were one of the few people who never gave up on me." "You'll have fun. Lia is amazing. I mean she puts up with Rawk, right?" While he calmed her fears I turned to Rawk.

"Am I doing the right thing Rawk? Every fibre of my being is telling me to stay with you but my head knows it's not safe for either of us if I do." "No it's not, look you read those reports, yeah and those are only what Rhy can clue together. Who knows what else that stupid cult is into?" We found out that Rawk's father is part of a weird businessman's elite club.

They are filthy rich, morally corrupt families who through the decades have answered to no social system of laws. If they do something...unsavoury they only have to explain it away to their elders and it got erased. It was incredible, if it was true. Don't get me wrong Rawk's father is a horrible man but I just couldn't believe he was capable of such evil.

Then again he is one of very few in the United Kingdom who are a part of the club. It was notoriously difficult to get in and even more so to stay in.

I nodded my head slowly and sighed, "I know I know I just-." "I know baby, fuck! I know." He pulled me into him and held me so tight I almost couldn't breathe.

"I got all of us onto a flight to France in 5 hours and from there the girls fly to the States." Rhys walked into the hotel room and told us. We decided not to go back to University until the very last minute in case someone was watching for us.

"I've spoken to David, he's thrilled, so if I'm not back in 5 days when university starts he'll cover for me," I replied to him and he exhaled. "Okay so we need to be at the airport in 3 hours, do what you gotta do before then. Rhys clarified before dropping down next to Chloe and pulling his tie off.

I pulled Rawk into our hotel room across the way. I was scared, sad, anxious and angry. I felt like I was in a dream, shit like this doesn't happen to real people. I focused on Rawk stripping his clothes off and all the other feelings were washed away by lust.

"Rawk I don't think I'm going to be able to sleep without you. I like waking up with your body wrapped around mine?" I whispered into his ear as I slid my pants off and my hands up along the sides of his neck. Then I stood up on my tiptoes to kiss him. "Jesus, dangerous Amarelia, what am I gonna do with you?" "Anything you want." I purred back, pushing him onto the bed and straddling him. His bulge tapped the heat of my wet centre each time I circled my hips.

He sat up and lifted me with one arm around my waist. Before I could squeak I was under Rawk and his lips were pressed into mine. His arm was still around my waist and when he lifted it my back arched into him. He pulled away from our kiss and looked at me "I love you." As the last word left his lips he pushed into me and I sighed in relief. "I love you too Rawk oh God."

Each time he pumped his arm it arched my back into him. He slammed all the way into me over and over. Little moans became gasps and soon Rawk had a hand over my mouth as he brought me to a spine-tingling orgasm. We dropped into a heap on the bed, set an alarm for an hour and slept. I knew that it may be the last time for a while so I held onto him extra tight.

FLY AWAY FROM ME

RAWK'S POV

I've never experienced a connection like this with anyone before, we were completely in sync and now I had to leave her. We dressed in silence and the drive to Uni was mostly the same. I was straight out afraid. I was afraid of not having her around, I was afraid of losing her completely. Mostly I was afraid she wouldn't come back. The guilt from that thought made it ten times worse. I knew she wouldn't be able to just leave me but the slither of a chance haunted me. My ma and Carys left me so why not her too.

We went to hers first, as it was further from the parking and we were leaving my car at the University. While she grabbed a bag of toiletries and clothes I called my grandparents.

"Hello nan," I said cheerfully, not wanting to go right in. "Rawk oh my darling how are you, when are you coming to visit again. I miss you?" She asked in her slightly accented English and I had to grin.

"How about today?" "Magnifique! Is anyone coming along?" "Um yeah, Rhys is coming." "Carys's cousin?" "Yes, nan we have some um business to talk with you about." "Well, then I look double forward to your visit, see you soon darling." I ended the call and went to find Amarelia.

"Yeah, Aki tomorrow morning I'm so excited! A field assignment with my friend Chloe, you'll love her." She rubbed her forehead side to side. I knew how much she hated to lie. "Okay, I'll see you then, love you." She disconnected and grabbed her bags.

"Right let's get this over with." She looked at me with such determination. I blocked her way and held her face in my hands. "We are not letting go yeah." My eyes penetrated into hers "Never." She answered fiercely and held out her pinky finger to me.

Our trip to the airport and flight to France went by without a hitch but I found myself unable to let go of Amarelia's hand when her flight was called for boarding. "Hey let it be an incentive to get this sorted as soon as possible. I know Rhys feels the same as you, he's literally just got Chloe back." She reasoned and I sighed again. "I know God I'm gonna miss you so much." "I love you Rawk." She murmured then kissed me goodbye.

"I love you Rawk." I gave his hand one last squeeze then kissed him goodbye. As I turned Chloe's red-rimmed eyes met mine and we linked arms. "This fucking sucks." Chloe shook her head slowly. "I know Chlo, I know." My voice broke and we clung to each other tighter.

The flight was made more comfortable by our first-class seats but I couldn't calm my racing thoughts. In my head I went back over all the paperwork Rhys had gathered, there was so much ridings on the next few days. They would decide how long Chloe and I had to stay away for. How long Connor and his cult of miscreants would go to jail for and, most importantly, whether Rawk would come out unharmed. The last thought sank my stomach. I couldn't imagine my world without him in it.

"Ami wami!!!" Akia's loud screech turned the heads of most of the waiting area. "And that's my sister, sorry." I apologised to Chloe, who was looking at Aki in bewildered awe. Before I could warn her Akia had both of us in a tight hug. "Oh my God, it's so good to see you! You must be Chloe, hi." Chloe's face split into a grin. "Hi, great to meet you. Apologies for getting you out of bed so early." "Are you kidding, as much as I tease I was so excited to see this one I hardly slept. Come on Leila is waiting in the car."

Leila and Chloe found common ground and chatted nonstop until we got to the hotel. "Please don't apologise, Leila, the department is paying for our stay at the hotel." I fibbed but I could stomach the lie because I knew that it would a) stop Leila and Akia from feeling bad and b) allow us privacy for when Rawk or Rhys made contact. There was a very afraid slither of me that also had an option c) what if Rawk's father found out where we were? I needed my family to be safe.

Akia and Leila hung around and had breakfast with us in the hotel. "How's work Ak?" I asked her while generously buttering a slice of toast. "It's so great, I'll take you guys to see it if you want." She beamed. Leila looked at her and smiled softly. It was a look of pure adoration. I was happy that she made my sister so happy. It was hard without Aki around but seeing how *alive* she was here made it acceptable.

"Did she tell you that her boss moved her to his flagship health centre?" Leila squeezed her hand and she blushed. "I still say Ari had something to do with it." "She is a very satisfied customer. Her feedback is as valid as any." Leila shot back with a smirk. "Who is Ari?" I asked. "It's my boss's wife, she's amazing. Just found out she's pregnant with her fourth kid."

"I think I'd also be permanently pregnant if I were married to her husband," Leila mumbled to Chloe but Aki's brows lifted. "Excuse me?" She crossed her arms over her chest and Leila cringed. "Even you have to admit he is a very well put together man, on all levels." She questioned. "Yeah, he is." She puffed air out and started laughing. Soon the whole table joined. It felt so good to relax.

They left after, making plans to see us again. As soon as we got into our room we went for our devices. "Anything?" I questioned. "YES! Oh thank God, they are okay. They saw Adaline and showed her what Rhys has compiled. She put them in contact with the investigator who is doing some digging for her.

They may have to fly out of the UK to meet him though." She read off the screen and gasped.

"Shit!" We both swore. "That exposes them for Finch." I hissed and she nodded. My insides turned to toffee. Rawk had said *not* to contact them and I understood why but it was so hard. I needed to know that he was okay. I needed to hear his voice.

I needed him.

CRAVINGS

RAWK'S POV

I felt numb. I couldn't get the sound of her voice out of my head, her gravelly laugh, her beautiful smile. Fuck I craved her. By the time we got to my grandmother's dance school, I had collected myself and given Rhys the low down on what Amarelia and I had discussed in Ireland.

"Mon chérie!" Adaline Guillem is not your average grandmother. I smiled widely as she glided toward us. For a woman well into life, she still looks incredible. I suppose all the years of dancing have paid off...or maybe it's the ageless Japanese genetics. "Hi nan, you remember Rhys." I double kissed her cheeks then shuffled Rhys forward. "Ah yes, you were the one who stuck bubble gum in that poor girl's hair." I snort laughed and Rhys coloured a deep shade of red.

"Um yes, Nicole hated me for ages after that." We all laughed at the memory. "The only reason she forgave you is that you got Ian to stop calling her sticky Nicky," I recalled fondly. She led us through the dance school and toward her office. "They are literally undressing you with their eyes," Rhys whispered with a chuckle. I just shook my head.

"So tell me what is this business we have to discuss?" My grandmother asked. "Rhys has been putting together as much as he can to build a case against my father and Finch." I started. "And I made an interesting discovery that has begun tying loose ends together." Rhys handed her the report on the 'Elite Businessman's Club'. "Merde!" My nan swore so I knew it was bad. "We must call Monsieur Priest immediately." She reached for her mobile and a loud ring soon blared from the speaker.

"Hello" An American accent answered. "Murray it is Adaline, how are you?" "In truth, I've been better." "Oh, no are you unwell?" "I broke my knee training with my nephew" "Oh no but this is terrible!" "I've had worse, I'll survive. What may I do for you, did you receive my update?" " Yes, I received it thank you. I have my grandson with me. Some news has come to light. Do you have time to talk at the moment?" She asked and a follow-up Facetime call was scheduled.

We made our way back to her house and exchanged findings over lunch. When Murray called we stood in my grandfather's office and exchanged information. After Rhys and Murray discussed the practicality of things and how to approach the law system with it Murray dropped the bomb.

"As much as I would love to fly over there immediately Adaline I won't be allowed due to the swelling of my leg." His face was a combination of frustration and guilt. All our

165

faces mimicked his. This was a setback we couldn't afford. "We could come to you?" Rhys offered suddenly. "Yes you could, Jacque is the apartment available?" She asked my grandfather.

"If it is not then it will be by the time they arrive. Use the jet Rawk, the quicker we get those bastards behind bars the better." My grandfather has never liked my father, he always felt my mother deserved better. He was right. "Would that work for you, Mr Priest?" I asked. "Murray, and I agree with your grandfather, we need to get this going ASAP. How soon can you leave? I am homebound for the next few weeks. Your distraction will be welcome." We discussed our plans with him and then with my grandparents.

Later I asked Rhys to message Chloe. There was no way my father would know her number so it seemed like the safest option. I had to let Amarelia know that I was okay. I ached to speak to her. We ate with my grandparents then got ready to leave.

"I wish I could speak to Chloe." Rhys huffed out, his hands raking through his hair. I knew exactly how he felt, I craved Amarelia's touch. "I feel you but they're safe yeah." "Yeah, it just sucks. I didn't think we'd get close again. She was so fucked up afterwards Rawk. She told me you visited her from time to time." He said in a low voice and I smiled at the memory.

"I always felt like it was my fault. If we hadn't been arguing or if I hadn't gotten so fucked

that night. Then I started digging into everything and the guilt, Rhys, it ate at me. The way I handled things was so fucking stupid. I loved Carys and I just let everything go to shit." I confessed and it felt good to get it off my chest to him.

"I'm guessing it took Amarelia a couple of lectures to get you to realise that it isn't your fault." I let out a single loud laugh at that. "Something like that yeah." "She's an incredible woman Rawk." "I know and that's why we need to get this right." My voice was hoarse with exhaustion and against what I believed possible I passed out for a few hours before the tingles of a nightmare woke me.

I watched the landscape enlarge as the plane dropped to land. Murray was obviously unable to collect us but he insisted that his nephew would. We walked out and immediately I knew who he was from the description. "Kit Forrester?" I asked, "Hi, welcome to America." He shook our hands and made small talk while we walked to his car.

"So minor detail, Murray probably didn't mention. This is my wife's car and she is at my gym. I just need to drop it off and collect mine, sorry guys." "No problem you're doing us a solid by collecting us yeah," I replied. That explained the size of the guy and maybe the bruises." You box?" I asked, "The bruises are compliments of my last fight, dickhead got a liberty in that nearly put me on my ass."

167

"Prick." "Cunt." Rhys and I exclaimed and the car erupted in laughter.

We arrived at the gym and I was impressed. I've always trained but this was more, it was an entire health centre. "Follow me, I'll introduce you to the Mrs." He led us upstairs into a spa. "Hey, Kensi is Ari done yet?" He asked a pretty California blonde behind the desk.

"Hi boss, she is but she went down to 'Squeeze'. She says she's craving peanut butter and banana smoothies." Kensi wiggles her eyebrows and giggled at Kit's face. "Oh God, please tell me that smoothies are gonna be the craving for this pregnancy. When she was pregnant with our twins she took to dipping fries in milkshake. " He said with disgust. Rhys and I both shrugged. "Standard practice." Rhys said and laughed at his horrified face. "That's just wrong. Thanks, Kensi, see you later." He walked us back down and toward a little smoothie and snack bar.

"You guys want anything. Honestly Ari's gonna force you to try something so you may as well get something you'll actually like." He warned walking up to the counter. We ordered what we wanted to try and Kit disappeared into the back to find his wife.

The woman that walked back out was an absolute knockout. Long, long dark hair and bright grey-blue eyes. "Hi I'm the Mrs but please call me Ari." She gave both of us a huge smile. We introduced ourselves and made our way out of the gym. On the way, I recalled what Murray told us.

"So how did your uncle end up with a broken knee?" Kit grimaced and Ari narrowed her eyes at him. "In my defence, he was going all military black ops on me. He said to go all in!" He replied more to his wife than us. "Yeah, and nobody puts Baby in a corner right." She teased him and he rolled his eyes at her.

"I have to go fetch the kids from my mom, are you guys joining us for dinner later?" She asked, starting her Subaru. "Not sure, we need to go see Murray." "Well, then I will probably see you later. Nice to meet you."

UNDER THE RAINBOW

For the next two days, we were drip-fed information from the boys and I was so frustrated that I wanted to scream. They'd left the UK in order to meet a guy named Murray Priest. Adaline and Jacque had hired him to do some private investigating for them. He had friends at Interpol and in the military. He also made some interesting connections regarding the Elite Club.

Chloe and I took Akia up on her offer and went to check out her new workspace. I was so proud of her, it was gorgeous. We met Ari, the bosses wife and she demanded that we come to the opening party she had planned for later. We agreed on a time and headed to the mall to find something suitable to wear. It was good to be distracted for a few hours.

"What do you think?" Chloe pulled the dressing room curtains apart and stepped out. "Daaymn!" The guy behind the counter whistled low and Chloe blushed a deep red. "Yeah what he said, Chlo you look hot. That's your dress babe!" I grinned madly at her. I know this is only the beginning of our friendship but I had a feeling we would be friends for many years to come.

While she hunted down heels to match I tried on a dress that reminded me of one I'd worn on the day I met Rawk. "Oh wow, Lia that's so beautiful! God, I wish I was as skinny as you." "What, don't be daft you are smoking hot. Now, what do you think of this dress with my thigh high boots?" I usually only wore them with a pair of jeans but the dress was so pretty, unfortunately, it was also short and I did not feel like fake tanning so thigh highs it would be.

"Ari is a fucking magician, what the hell?" Leila marvelled. "I know isn't it incredible! She got all this done in an afternoon." The room was festooned with black and gold balloons and banners. Music played softly through the system and tables overflowed with finger foods. "Oh my God Lia try this this dol...dolo just put it in your mouth." Chloe tried to pronounce the Greek word but gave up and shoved the stuffed vine roll into my mouth.

"Oh my God, it tastes just like my aunt's *dolmas*." I groaned when I took another bite and Chloe pulled me along to the next table. "I want to marry whoever made this and have their children." Chloe purred savouring the taste of her coconut and peach sauce ice cream. "My aunt would take that as the greatest compliment." Ari popped up beside us with Leila and Aki.

"This is all just incredible Ari." Leila gushed. "She deserves every bit of recognition, you are an incredible therapist." She answered genuinely. "Oh stop." Aki dismissed. Just then a tiny human came barrelling into my leg. "I sorry, mama mama look." The boy was beautiful; he had his mother's dark hair and bright blue eyes.

"I'm sorry but Dominic has no chill. Look at what bug?" She picked the boy up and he held his little hand up. "My hand, I got box hand like daddy." All of us leaned in to look at the bruise then looked back up as one.

"Crap, okay hold on, beautiful I can explain. It's not what it looks like." A massive guy strolled up to us with a slightly older boy on his shoulders. "Kit, what the hell?" Her eyes shot daggers at him and I couldn't control my giggle. That set Kit and his shoulder pal off.

"He wanted to know why Pete can do karate and he can't so I agreed that he could do the warm-ups with us. He faces planted on the first bow and caught his hand on a corner." Ari looked to Pete for confirmation and he nodded. "It's true mama the roar was there too."
"Roar?" Ari asked looking between the three of them.

I heard a familiar voice call Chloe's name. Oh my God! "Rhys?" I asked aloud but Chloe was gone. She was halfway across the room in seconds. I was so shocked to see Rhys that what it meant hadn't clicked yet. "My wife and I put two and two together yesterday. Murray Priest is my uncle." Kit explained when I turned to him.

I was frozen to the spot. All I could do was watch Rawk stalk toward me. He wasn't alone for long though. A little girl gripped onto his hand and he hoisted her up into his arms. My ovaries exploded or hormones or clock or whatever it is that makes you want a baby.

Rawk with a child was sexy AF! "Good lord, who is that?" Leila asked. "My research partner," I answered and Aki's brows shot up.

The little girl climbed from Rawk's arms into her fathers and distracted the others while Rawk walked us slightly back. He held my face in his hands and locked eyes with me. "Promise me we won't be apart after this yeah. I can't do it again baby, I want you with me. " He mumbled before kissing me hard. When we came up for air I ran my fingers along his jaw. "Kissing you is like finding the treasure under the rainbow." It was cheesy but true.

"Fuck I love you Amarelia and I love this dress." He rumbled against my ear and I felt his hand slide down my back and grope my butt. "Wanna take it off me?" I asked in response walking past him to the toilets. His face lit up with a smirk and he followed closely. We barely made it in before Rawk had me against the wall.

The door shut behind us and we kissed furiously. Someone cleared their throat and it took me a few seconds to come out of my trance. "Oh, shit Rawk." I hissed at him, giggles erupting at random. He opened his eyes. Lined up along the mirror were at least 5 women, all watching. Rawk pulled the back of my dress down and we turned to leave. I was trying my hardest not to go into full-blown nervous laughter attack.

"Excuse us ladies. I haven't seen my girl in 3 days." He motioned for me to lead the way and

I heard the woman erupt into giggles and comments. "We need to leave, NOW!" His voice was hoarse against my hair and I felt heat pool at my centre. "What about Chloe and Rhys?" "Trust me Rhys wants to leave too, let's go grab them."

We hung around for Kit's speech then said our goodbyes. Rawk couldn't keep his hands to himself so by the time we got to the apartment I was a mess. "So this is your grandparent's place?" Chloe asked when we walked in. "Yeah, my grandfather does a lot of business in the States so it made sense to buy a place instead of staying in hotels. It's safer too." Rawk answered.

As soon as the bedroom door shut behind us I was back up against a wall. "I need you inside me, right now!" I said into Rawk's mouth and felt his cock twitch against my stomach. "Fuckin hell woman." He hissed then hoisted me up by the back of my thighs. My arms linked around his neck and I pulled his mouth onto mine. He circled one arm around my waist and I locked my ankles around him. A finger brushed over my thong and a shudder passed through me. "I can feel how wet you are through these." He slid his finger slowly along the seam of the fabric and I had to bite my lip not to moan.

"Why are you feeling through them?" I purred innocently and watched Rawk's eyes dilate with lust. He walked us over to a chair and sat me down. "These need to come off first." He lifted one leg then the other and slid my boots off. I stood when he turned and popped the buttons on his jeans. Soon we were both naked and he picked me up again.

"I dreamt about this last night." He whispered in my ear just before I felt his tip line up with my very exposed centre. I gasped softly and pushed down. "I love you Amarelia." He told me then pulled my butt forward forcing himself inside me. "I love you Rawk," I answered then got lost in him pounding into me.

RAWK'S POV

Waking up with Amarelia in my arms was everything I'd dreamt about. I smirked when I noticed her lacy thong still hooked on the corner of the chair. I doubt I'll ever get enough of her. I tried to get up without waking her but she rolled over immediately and patted the bed. "No, where are you going?" She mumbled. "To make us a coffee." "Hmmm okay."

"Thank you." She took the mug with a smile." You are very welcome." I teased and watched her cheeks light up. We sat on the balcony and enjoyed our coffee. We knew life was going to be rough when we got back. We weren't meant to be in a relationship and I'd basically asked her to quit her life and choose me....and she had, now this, fuck! I was nervous, my father hadn't left North Manor but according to Ian and Siobhan, many people had come to see him. He had something up his sleeve.

"Are you okay?" She stood in front of me tapping my foot with hers. She was so perfect. I had to make sure she was safe. "Just thinking about the best way to get back home." I spread my arms and she sat on my lap, curling into me. "I fucking love you." "I love you." She giggled against my chest. We stayed like that, enjoying the silence until Chloe called for breakfast.

"Do we have a plan for getting back to London? Wait when are we going back?" Chloe asked. Rhys and I shared a look before he sighed heavily. "We have to go see Murray

176

this morning. There are a few last things to sign off on before our plan can be set in motion. "And what is the plan?" She narrowed her eyebrows at him. "Honestly Chlo the less you know about it the safer you'll be in the long run." I interrupted their glare off and the seriousness of the situation settled around us.

"Chloe and I could go visit my grandparents with Aki while you two are doing that? Murray's team did the security for my grandparent's house. Aki told them about the break-in last year and Ari asked Murray to help. They really are an incredible family." She was nervous and rambling. "That's a great idea baby." I interrupted her and she swallowed.

Aki and Chloe reminisced about the party along the way while I watched the houses and trees dip and weave. It was so good to see my grandparents and soon they absorbed us into a cocoon of laughter and memories. "What a wonderful surprise!" "Yes, the best. Are you sure you can't stay for dinner?" Gran pouted but I was saved by my ringing mobile.

I mouthed a sorry and stuck my finger in the air before I answered. All their eyes followed me. I smiled tightly and walked out of the room. "Hello." "Hey, baby." Rawk's voice had the power to buckle my knees. "Hi." I breathed out "Murray contacted Scotland Yard and they were very interested in what we had to say, so we have our plan. I'll tell you more when I come to get you. I wanna come get you now. Where are you?"

There was something in his strained voice, *panic*, something was wrong. I stopped pacing the terrace. "Rawk you can tell me to fuck off but are you okay okay?" "I'm a fine baby I just need to come get you yeah." Anxiety washed across me in a wave.

"Rhys has the address. I'll see you soon." I tried to stay calm but it felt like I had a balloon in my throat. "Yeah." He clipped out. "Rawk?" "Yeah." "Am I okay?" I whispered and heard something shatter before he swore. "Don't let anyone in. I'll see you soon yeah." His voice was hoarse and he left me with no answers so either he was angry or scared. For the first time, I sincerely hoped it was anger.

I needed a minute before I went back in. I locked myself in the guest loo and practised the breathing exercises Dr Lee taught me. When I could face myself in the mirror again I straightened out and joined the others. Chloe saw right through my smile and gave me a curious look. I shook my head as subtly as I could.

When the doorbell rang Chloe and I jumped up. "Well, that's our ride." I hugged my family and tugged Chloe to the door but Aki was faster and still had that big mouth on her.

"Is that Rawk in the car?" She asked me. "Yes." I glared at her. "Who's Rawk?" Grandad asked. "Her boyfriend." "What? Why would you not tell him to come in? Where are your manners, Lia?" Gran huffed and I wanted to slap the smirk off my sisters face.

"Oh shiittt." Chloe drew the word out and pointed at my gran. She had her head in the car. I stomped over and firmly tugged her back then asked Rawk to get out. He obeyed me without a fight all the while trying to keep the corners of his mouth down. My cheeks flared nonstop. "Rawk this is my gran Jo and my grandad Andy, this is Rawk."

I was going to faint with embarrassment. My gran had tears in her eyes. "Oh, it's such a pleasure to meet you. God, you're handsome and so strong. " She squeezed Rawks forearm like she was testing fruit. "Oh my God *gran!*" Rawk raised his brows at her "Well thank you."

"Oh and that accent. You must bring my granddaughter back this evening so we can all have dinner together?" She went in for the kill and Rawk's smile broke free. "I would love to. We leave in the morning so we can't stay too late but I can't wait to hear all your stories about her as a girl." His answer shocked me.

"Darling, why don't we go to Tia's, it's not fair that you cook all day long?" Grandad cast Aki and me urgent glances and we both stifled our giggles. "That's even better, closer to our hotel." I blurted out and my grandfather winked at me. "Oh alright, it has been quite a morning. See you at 6 then, bye darlings." Gran wrapped her arm around Aki as they walked back into the house and I knew she was getting cross-questioned. Serves her right.

"What's wrong with your gran's cooking?" Chloe asked. "It's fucking awful! Don't get me wrong she's the queen of desserts but she just cannot cook an actual meal. Once she tried to roast a chicken and somehow the end of the kitchen towel got stuck in the oven. She almost burnt the house down." We drove back to the apartment and I could feel Rawk winding up like a coil. He kept squeezing my fingers. Almost as if he was checking that I was still there.

As soon as we got in Rhys pulled Chloe away, leaving us alone. "Hi." I pulled my head back and stood on my tippy toes to kiss him. His hands went around my waist and squeezed. "You alright?" He asked automatically and I zoned my eyes into his. "You're not alright though?" I watched him wrestle with himself.

"Siobhan called. Apparently Finch went to pay Chloe a visit and gleefully reported his findings to my father." "Fuck so what now?" The balloon in my throat expanded a little more. "It's better that we're out tonight. We are leaving tomorrow but not together. You and Chloe fly out two hours after us. Rhys and I will go to yours and grab your stuff. We're having a sleepover at Rhys's until this is over."

"Okay is there anything you need to tell me?" I was buying time while I digested what he said. "No, I don't wanna talk Amarelia I just can we please just chill." He turned me around but kept a hold of my waist. Then led us to his bed and pulled me into his arms. "I just need you to be safe yeah." He held me almost too tight against him, he was scared.

We met at *Tia Soborosa* and it was a whole different level of chaos. Ari has more family than me and that's saying something. The evening was a great reprise although Rawk stayed my shadow at all times, which didn't do much to calm my nerves. His nightmares kept us awake most of the night so the journey to the airport was quiet. Rawk kept his hand on the small of my back until it was time for them to leave. Two hours later we boarded and were both asleep within an hour of the flight ascending

YOUR MOVE

RAWK'S POV

"Who is this?" I growled into my mobile. Nothing annoys me more than a private number. "Aww, Rawk is that any way to speak to your father?" His raspy voice made the hairs on the back of my neck stand and my blood ran cold. "What do you want?" I responded neutrally and he sniggered. "Just wondering where you've been? You created such a shit storm here then disappeared into thin air." "What do you care where I am? I was in France." "Ah, and how are Adaline and Jacque?" "Grand." I spat out

"Funny thing is Chloe Stone also disappeared for a few days along with Rhys. You wouldn't happen to know where Rhys is, would you?" I shot my eyes to him and he told me to put the call on speaker so he could record it. "Even if I do know where Rhys is why would I tell you? What do you want with him?" "I thought he'd be interested to know who I'm on my way to see. I gather from the visitor logs and release forms that she's fucking him." He hissed over the phone and my knees buckled

"What do you mean on the way to see?" I asked the question I didn't want the answer to. "Oh come now Rawk I know you're smarter than that. Hmm, she really has such a beautiful face that girl of yours reminds me a bit of your

*mother. Anyway, I'll be sure to say hi to them."
The line disconnected.*

*When we arrived earlier we got an Uber to the
University from the airport. I got what we
needed from our rooms and got my car then we
went straight to Rhys's. We were waiting for
the girls to arrive. Amarelia had messaged me
when they arrived and said they were getting
into an Uber. My father called 15 minutes after
that. "What the fuck happened? FUCK!" I
roared and kicked the kitchen counter. "Does
he mean..." Rhys's face went slack as
realisation set in. "We need to call Murray,
NOW."*

*Rhys spoke to Murray while I tried to control
my temper. That fucking dickhead had
Amarelia. I let her out of my sight and my
worst fear had become reality. "If you think
Interpol can help. Oh oh, I didn't think yes
okay. I'll send you the recording." Rhys
disconnected and walked over to me. He
squeezed my shoulder and pointed at his front
door. "Where are we going?" "To get our
girls back and end the fuckers that dared to
touch them." I was terrified of what I was
capable of doing in this mood but I nodded and
followed him out.*

"Not gonna lie that's the best sleep I've had in
days." Chloe stretched as we waited to get our
carry-on luggage down. "Wow me too. Rawk
was having nightmares last night." "Still? He
used to get them when we were younger after

his mum and all happened. It used to freak Carys out." "Do you mind talking about her? Rawk told me bits but it still hurts him." "Nah I don't mind." "What was she like, before… everything."

Chloe gave me a sad smile. "Carys, Siobhan and Nicole were legends in our little town. They were badass bitches. Vicky and I copied everything they wore, went everywhere they did. They were always cool to us. Until that one night, things were perfect." She shook her head and swallowed back tears.

"I'm sorry Chloe you don't have to talk about it." "No, it actually feels good to. Did Rawk tell you that his aunt's stepson was one of the guys who raped us?" "Yeah, he explained the family tree a bit. I can't believe Damon would do that. Actually, I'm lying I can, he's a dick."

"Huh you know I thought my parents not believing me was the worst part then I believed Damon threatening a repeat performance was the worst part. But the real worst part was Vicky overdosing followed by Carys dying. I was so scared. The only reason I even tried was Rhys visiting me. Rawk and Nicole came too but it was too painful for him. I was everything he failed at."

I sent Rawk a text to let him know we were getting into our Uber after finally getting out. I couldn't wait to see him. The traffic flowed so we were making good time. Not good enough to get us pulled over so I was shocked when the blue lights flashed behind us. Our driver, Gary, shot us a confused look.

"Good afternoon officer, is something wrong?" Gary asked. "Routine checks, licence please." He asked with a smile and my nerves calm a little. "I'll just run these." He told Gary and ran his eyes across Chloe and I. All three of us watched as he got back into his car and spoke into his two way. His face broke into a smirk before he nodded.

"Hey Gary, what's his name?" I asked something was niggling at me. "Badge said Finch, O Finch." "Fuck!" Both Chloe and I cursed under our breaths. "Gary I need you to do me a favour. Just listen to me. When he comes back he's going to have a reason for separating you from us." Gary started to protest but Chloe shushed him, ordering him to just listen.

"I am putting my phone in your centre console. As soon as you can I want you to retrieve it and press 3. Explain everything in as much detail as you can. Now act natural. " I shoved my knee in the back of his seat as Finch leaned against the roof of the car and grinned.

"We seem to have a bit of a problem Mr Jones. You need to report to your head office immediately. I will be happy to take these young ladies to their final destination." I moved my knee around and Gary snapped into his role. "What oh no way, sorry ladies no clue what is going on. Thanks, officer." Gary played his part to the max. Chloe shot me a panicked look before we both got out.

Finch carried our luggage and tossed it into the back of his police car. When he turned I saw Gary snap a photo of the plates. I turned to have one last look and he had my phone to his ear. My breath wasn't filling my lungs properly and I started feeling faint. Where was he taking us? Chloe gripped my hand painfully and it brought me back. We kept our heads down and Finch stayed quiet.

"Yes sir on the way now. Elite Ealing, thank you, sir, I'll let them know." He said into his mobile then his eyes caught mine in the rear view mirror. "Connor says Rawk is not very happy at the moment." He had the audacity to chuckle. I called his bluff and smiled back widely in response. "Where are you taking us?" He narrowed his eyes for a second.

"Why?" "Just wondering how long it's going to take Rawk to find me and rip your spine out." I went for shock value and judging from how he paled I knew I'd hit a sore spot. He was afraid of Rawk. Why was he doing this than, did Connor have something on him or..."Are you kidnapping us for Connor or for the Elite club?" I asked and his fingers immediately tightened around the steering wheel. Fuck that answered that question.

"Sit tight you're about to find out sweetheart." His eyes went completely blank and Chloe clutched my fingers in her death grip. Rawk

would find me. I just kept telling myself
that...Rawk would find us.

HIDE & SEEK

RAWK'S POV

When my mobile rang again, not 10 minutes after my father's call, Rhys and I stared it down. The caller ID said it was her and that made dread settle in on me. "Amarelia?" "No, this is Gary Jones, I was their Uber driver." "How do you have her phone then?" "She hid it in my car and asked me to call you as soon as I could. Excuse my rudeness but what the hell is going on here?" Gary asked hesitantly.

"It's a long fucking story and there is no time to explain. I need you to tell me everything you recall yeah." My tone was sharp "Sure, I got the plates to officer Finch's police car, there's footage on my dashcam too." I was grateful this guy had been their driver. Most other people would have freaked out and gone straight to the cops.

"Finch! Oliver that little fucker. Don't worry Gary I know exactly how to find him." I growled. At the same time, something that had been bothering me finally made sense. Rhys took over and got all the details while I stalked up and down the room doing math. We agreed to meet for Amarelia's phone.

Rhys and I were both deep in our own thoughts while I drove. We spoke to Murray and an investigator from Scotland Yard. We were meeting him once I got the phone. After some time I broke the silence with a question. "Is there a possibility that Oliver and Damon are part of the Elites or at least trying to be?" "Like pledges?" He turned wide eyes on me. "Yeah exactly." "Holy shit!"

We drove through the streets of London in silence. Chloe nudged me and pointed. "That used to be an asylum back in the day." I followed her finger toward a huge sign that said ***St. Bernard's gate***.

"Clever girl, they teach you that while you were locked away sweetheart?" His tone was mean. I couldn't understand why he was so angry. He laughed quietly as we drove through the complex.

Oliver ordered us out and made a call. "Yes, sir we are outside North House right now. To the suite yes sir." He signalled at the door and we shuffled in. "Welcome to North House. This used to house the doctors that worked at the crazy house now it houses the Elite." He looked proud and it made my stomach roll.

"What are *we* doing here?" Chloe asked after we'd been frisked and ordered to sit. "Worried about what we're gonna do with you sweetheart?" Oliver replied with a sickening grin on his face. "Oh, I remember just what you like to do *sweetheart.*" Disgust filled her eyes. His smile faltered but he covered it up quickly with a snort.

"What the fuck are you on about?" "What was it you said to Vicky the night you raped her? Something about being fucked by the law?" Chloe's eyes filled with tears and she clenched her jaw hard to stop them from falling. "No one would believe you, you crazy fucking slut and there's no evidence anyway." He stood over Chloe but she never shrank back, she was so brave.

"Yeah, but this time the truth is involved. There's evidence and the case won't be put before Judge Coleman." "Shut up you don't know what the fuck you're talking about." He huffed. "But *I* do and she's right you're fucked. You and the rest of the Elites." I added my two cents and watched Oliver lose his cool.

His breathing got heavy and before I knew what was happening he had slapped me across the face. "Rawk is going to fucking kill you." "He better hurry up then, Connor will be here soon." He didn't sound as confident as before and I had just realised something. There was a knock at the door. Oliver went to answer it and I turned to Chloe.

"If Damon raped you and Oliver raped Vicky then who raped Carys?" "Damon raped Carys." "So he raped both of you?" "Yeah, Damon wasn't the first to rape me though I don't recall much from the beginning because I was pretty out of it. All I remember is that the first guy wore this really overpowering cologne but there's nothing else."

Connor walked in, looking in much better health than I'd seen him the last time. "Well well Chloe Stone, you're a slippery little one aren't you and Lia, how lovely to see your face again." His eyes slid over Chloe and me before he smirked. "This is Aleksy, one of my associates from the Polish Elites. He very kindly keeps an eye on North House and you two will be his guests until your time is up."

"You won't get away with this." Chloe hissed at him. "Ah but I will. Lucky for you Lincoln Black is no longer around or this would have all been over so much faster." "That's the guy who was part of a trafficking ring. I remember the case." I mumbled then the connection hit me, Ari. "Yes fine young man with so much potential. One of the best pledges American Elites have had in years." "You're sick." I shook my head in disbelief at what he was saying.

"So what now, you gonna drug us and sell us to the sex trade?" Chloe was scared and the words just blurted out of her. "Sex trade good God no that's never been my thing. No, before I dispose of Rhys's witness Aleksy is going to teach you a lesson about shutting up. You seem to have a problem with that." Connor ran his finger down Chloe's jaw.

"And you, you remind me of her. Maybe that's why my son is so stuck on you. He never got over her. She always chose him." "I remind you of Carys?" Rawk never went into detail about her looks but Nicole said she had Rhys's colouring. He was a gingery blonde with bright blue eyes.

"Not Carys, Charlotte, his mother. I guess it's too bad he doesn't get to keep either of you." He whispered, pushing a piece of my hair behind my ear. He leaned in and tugged his fingers down sharply. My head pulled horribly to the side and I yelped in pain. "I got rid of Charlotte out of necessity and this is no different. It's nothing personal but you have to die. Both of you. I have big plans and I've come too far for them to be ruined by a lunatic and a flavour of the month." He let go of my hair and I rubbed my scalp, trying to soothe the sting.

"Before you two meet your untimely death in an awful car accident I have questions. Ah, wonderful Piotr is here." He turned as the door behind us opened and in walked a heavily tattooed, incredibly intimidating looking guy. "Connor, sorry I'm late I went to see Moretti." He nodded "Piotr, no problem, welcome you're just in time for Q & A." As he spoke he unpacked a bag.

There were an old fashioned voice recorder and a pen next to a pad of paper. Then a roll of duct tape came out followed by rope. I shared a teary look with Chloe. Rawk really needed to get here soon. I was officially shitting myself.

STATE OF THE GAME

RAWK'S POV

We got Amarelia's phone and Gary's details then made our way to meet detective Campbell from Scotland Yard. He was a tightly packed man with an overgrown moustache that he enjoyed twirling.

"So you're able to link them all up?" Rhys questioned. "We are now thanks to your evidence. You'd make a damn great detective lad." "What's the link?" I asked, my patience were thin at best and I just wanted to find Amarelia. Every minute that ticked by was another she spent with those bastards.

"The Elite Club. Everything goes back to it. The property, the money, the drugs, the trafficking. All of it comes back to the Elites." "So they are obviously much more organised than a little gang of arseholes," Rhys commented and Campbell laughed. "Yes, in fact, they are more of an international cartel that has fingers in more pies than you can imagine." He excused himself when his doorbell chimed.

"So why the fuck is he moving his shit into my mother's name?" I hissed at Rhys as soon as the detective disappeared. "Maybe he doesn't trust the Elites as much as he'd like them to believe." "Sounds about right for the old cunt. I'm going to call Siobhan and tell her to get

her ma and brother away from North Manor."
"Good idea."

"Hello." "Nicky, it's me are you with Shiv?"
*"Jesus Rawk yeah we're at the Manor. What
the fuck is going on? There are people
crawling all around here. They're carrying out
files and destroying papers." She whispered
and I clenched my jaw. "Shit's about to go
horribly south Nicky, I need you to get my aunt
and cousins and get the fuck out of there,
now!"*

*"Fuck okay. We'll go to Stu but...Peter is here.
He's been asking all these weird questions."
"Peter? When did he arrive?" "This morning,
he kept asking if I knew where Rhys was. Said
he had something important to discuss with
him." "Nicky you keep away from that fucker
yeah. He's part of this whole fucking mess and
he won't hesitate to hurt any of you if he has
to."*

*"Shit! I'll call you as soon as we are at Stu."
"Alright, stay alert yeah." She hesitated for a
bit before asking, "Rawk, did he have anything
to do with Carys and Chloe's rape? I've just
always had a feeling." "Damon, Oliver Finch
and Peter started the pledge programme just
before that night. You're a smart girl Nicky
what do you think?" "Motherfucking dick! I'll
call you soon." "Nicky quiet and safe, no one
knows we know yet."*

NICOLE'S POV

Rawk said quietly. Rawk said control. Rawk said FUCK THAT! I walked into the front room undetected. Peter was stood at the window while Siobhan and Ian argued with their mother. They wanted to go to Cardiff. I typed a message on my phone and handed it to Sara who then showed it to the siblings. When Ian went to protest I put my finger to my lips and shook my head then pointed toward Peter.

Whether it was the rolling nerves coming off me or the desperation in my eyes they all stopped shuffling and nodded. I sat with a huff and sighed. "My ma wants me to meet her for lunch at the centre, anyone wanna join me. Please come with Shiv, ooh Sara you should come too. Ma has been dying to tell you about her trip to France." I played it on thick.

"Why not, I'll go crazy sitting in this house all day." Siobhan slapped her thighs then stood. "Great so you guys are gonna just leave me here, that sucks, I'm going to Troy's then," Ian whined. Peter didn't even budge when we left the room. We crammed into my guest bedroom and I tried explaining as much as I could as quickly as I could.

"What the actual fuck are you saying?" Shivvy didn't want to believe it. "Nicky these are big accusations." Ian pushed the hair off his forehead and held it back in his fingers. "I know and if Rawk hadn't sounded like he was about to murder someone I would have been more sceptical too."

"But why do we have to get away from Peter...is he involved in this?" "They think he's a pledge. It's not definite-" I started but she cut me off mid-sentence, "Oh my God. For how long?" "Almost two years." "Who else?" The tears streamed down her face. "Oliver and Damon." "Ol, Oliver Finch and Damon Cole- oh my God! Oh my fucking God. PETER!!" I couldn't stop her, truth be told I didn't want to.

"What the fuck did you do you stupid prick? Why...oh my God she was like a fucking sister to me. You fucking piece of shit." It took Ian and me to restrain her. "What's your problem? I haven't touched a hair on Nicole's head, not my type, no matter what bullshit she claims." He laughed at us. "She's not talking about Nicole she means Carys."

Everything about Peter changed the second Ian said Carys's name. He paled and sat on the closest surface to him. "What are you on about?" He made a last attempt at ignorance. "You, Damon and Oliver. You three raped them, didn't you? Oh my God did you rape Carys?" Siobhan buckled forward and made an inhuman sound.

Peter walked to her, dropping to his knees. She flinched back in the couch but he grabbed her hands. "I never wanted that, I didn't touch Carys. I swear!" He looked so genuine and so damaged but Siobhan ripped her hands away from him like he was the fire. "You sick fuck." Her voice shook terribly. "I'm so sorry Shivvy it was meant to be easy. Lure someone away from a crowd undetected and get them to one of the Elite houses. That's all."

"Prove it, tell that to Rawk," I said and all eyes swung to mine. "No fucking way. Rawk will kill me and then I'll go to jail. I'm still black and blue from the last time with North." "What do you think the Elites will do to you?" Sara sniggered at Peter and he seemed to get smaller. "Fuck fuck fuck fuck." He slammed his fist into the floor beside him. "Call Rawk." He heaved out.

"Are you at Stuart's?" Rawk sounded relieved. "Um, no slight change of plan." Before I slid the phone away from my ear I told Rawk to record the conversation. "What's going on Nicky?" "Peter has something to tell you." My eyes bored into Peter's and he began.

He sang like a fucking bird. He never wanted to be a part of the Elites, he didn't have the stomach for it but the more involved he got with Siobhan's future and North Enterprises the more Connor pushed. He told them about the first pledge challenge and how Damon decided to make it personal because of Rawk.

How Jack had allowed Damon to see Chloe after the rape and how both of them had visited Vicky shortly before her overdose. How Oliver got rid of the evidence and Judge Coleman (Who was also an Elite member) threw the case out. Peter confessed that he had tried to rape Chloe but he couldn't do it so he chickened out and let the other two have their way while he got stupid drink instead.

"They wouldn't let me leave though. Not before I, I did it too, they said it was insurance. They were gonna pin it all on me if I didn't. Vicky was so out of it, the worst of the three so I, I oh Jesus I did it. I wish I could take it all back." "Well you can't but you can help me find Chloe and Amarelia now." Rawk's voice was beyond controlled and it made me shudder to imagine what he was going to do to the three of them.

"They have Chlo?" Siobhan shrieked. "Start thinking Peter or what Rawk can do to you will pale on comparison to what I'm capable of," I warned him. "What happened?" Peter asked Rawk and he explained. "Damn, smart girl, my best guess is that they took them to North House, it's on the old asylum grounds in Ealing. St. Bernard's gate, the top suite."

FUZZ HITS THE FAN

RAWK'S POV

We raced through traffic lights and cut across lanes as the GPS led us to the doors of St. Bernard's gate. Getting in was the easy part, I leaned over Detective Campbell and introduced myself. "My father is expecting me." I showed him my driver's license and used the tone I had fine-tuned over the years, complete disinterest and annoyance. It was my father's best.

"Sorry, sir please go through." The guard removed his hands from the car and we drove into the parking. Now for the tricky part. Damon was currently being arrested along with Judge Coleman and Chief Finch. Back up was on the way and I had so much pent up rage I reckon I could take out a good few guys on my own. But a lot was hanging on how much time we had before my father was made aware of what was happening and that was the tricky part.

The agent from Interpol stayed behind to contact his headquarters in Lyon. He tied two American drug dealers to the Elites. They were suspected of selling the cocaine that killed 4 kids in one night and a total of 26 over a weekend.

The fuzz was about to hit the fan on all fronts and Amarelia was in the middle of all of it, beside my psycho fucking father.

"Sir your son is on the way up." A voice came through the intercom on the wall. Rawk was here, I sagged back and Chloe squealed beside me. Connor had been asking ridiculous questions about Rawk's grandparents that I didn't know the answers to. I now understood why he never wanted to get me involved, the less I knew the better.

Chloe was laced into the chair beside me. Oliver duct-taped her then tied her down with ropes. They bit into her skin and the more she wriggled the more blood oozed from her wrists and ankles. I only had duct tape around my wrists but I didn't move around, I was too scared.

"What? How the fuck did he know where we are?" Oliver's eyes shot all around the room. He turned to me and I smiled quickly before looking down, "He's going to hurt you, all of you." My voice was low and the timing perfect, Rawk banged fiercely on the door. Aleksy and Piotr pulled out guns and backed away. Connor stood and smiled widely. "Who's there?"

"This is Detective Campbell from Scotland yard. You are under arrest Mr North." Connor's reaction was a picture. The two Polish guys took off, they scrambled out of the lounge window and down the fire escape stairs faster than Connor could call them out. There was another loud knock but Connor was suspended. Oliver grabbed a knife and started cutting Chloe and I free.

"Open this fucking door you sick cunt." Rawk roared through the door and Connor snapped out of it. The door flew back the second it was unlocked and Rawk almost walked through his father to get to me. "Amarelia!" "I'm fine, calm down, I'm fine but she needs a doctor." Rhys ran in and when he saw Chloe he marched over to Oliver.

"You think you're untouchable but I'm making sure that you're gonna get touched a whole lot." Then he turned to Chloe and gently held her to him. "Let's get you to the medic downstairs." He led her toward the lift and nodded at Rawk as he passed, I could see the relief in his face. Campbell had Connor and Oliver in cuffs. Piotr and Aleksy were caught trying to creep into the garage parking.

Soon Rawk and I were the only two left in the suite. We stood at the window with him wrapped around me and watched the scene below. Detective Campbell was joined by another guy, who had just driven in. "That's the guy from Interpol." Rawk told me.

"Oh, shit look." I pointed to the backdoor of a car. "Is that Peter?" I squinted. "Yeah, Nicky and Shivvy got him to roll on the Elites." "What now?" I was gobsmacked. "He claims he was forced into pledging by my father and into raping Vicky by Damon." "So he was the third guy." "Yeah."

"Holy shit this is insane." "I'm sorry Amarelia I never should have gotten you involved in this" He chewed on the inside of his bottom lip and shook his head. "Where's my phone?" I asked and he frowned in confusion. He pulled it out of his back pocket and handed it over. I went into my settings and changed him to number one on my speed dial.

"You are my fucking number one person you dickhead and if you ever say stupid shit like that again I'll leave your sorry ass." I pulled him down and kissed him hard. "I fucking love you." He mumbled against my lips.

My eyes caught movement below us. Two guys were running toward the crowd downstairs, they both had guns and masks on. "Oh, shit Rawk!" I shrieked but it was too late. The first shot was quiet, he must have had a silencer on, and Peter dropped like a stone. I heard Chloe's terrified scream but it was drowned out seconds later when the second gun fired in a loud explosion of sound. One two three shots rang out, I clapped my hands over my ears and buried my head in Rawk's chest. Time seemed to slow down for a few minutes.

"Oh my God, oh fuck, Jesus fuck!" Rawk swore, stiffening against me and when I tried to turn he held me tight in place. "Don't look, baby." He heaved out a breath and swallowed. "What happened? Are they okay?" I whispered, afraid of his answer. Chloe and Rhys came running through the door, she looked frantic. Rhys was trying to calm her down.

"It's okay Chlo you're okay." "No, I'm not oh my God did you see Peter they he's and Aleksy they're both dead aren't they?" She spewed words out before losing her knees and folding into Rhys's arms. "There were four shots fired," I stated with huge eyes.

"I'm sorry Rawk." Chloe wailed. "Your father? They shot him, is he?" I asked but Rawk shook his head so I turned to Rhys. "Yeah but he's still alive." "We need to go down Rawk." I tried to move but it was pointless. "I'm only taking you down after they've cleared off." His tone left no room for argument.

I called Nicole and caught them up. They were at Stuart's and would be safe there for now. I heard Siobhan swearing and Sara arguing about going to the hospital and turned to Rawk. He took my phone.

"Hey Nicky, yeah I know yeah thanks. Tell my aunt that I'll make sure they transfer him to the University hospital if he survives but I don't want anyone on the roads... actually put me on speakerphone." His voice was low and cold, he sounded like a stranger.

Voices burst through the line. "You lot need to shut up and listen to me yeah. No-one goes out alone, all of you make your way to North Manor and stay there, you too Stuart. Aunt

Sara, I need you to send all the staff home and make sure all the security systems are working. We are coming up as soon as we've been to the hospital." There were a few questions and arguments but we all agreed eventually; North Manor was where we would have the numbers and be the safest.

Campbell told us that Oliver and Piotr were in a holding cell and Connor was being rushed into surgery at the West Middlesex hospital. He would be under constant surveillance until it was possible to transfer him to jail. Peter's confession could still be used in court as he had insisted on signing it, almost as if he'd known he wouldn't be coming back.

"Also I apologise but I have to ask you a few questions before you leave." "Can't we do that in the morning?" Rawk snapped but I shook my head at him. "It's fine I'd rather get it over with," I assured him and gave the detective a small smile. After he heard all that happened we were allowed to leave.

Rawk called his grandparents and Murray while I gave my statement then we got an officer to give us a ride to Rawk's car. "What now?" Chloe asked. "Now we go see if my father's gonna live. Then we go wait in Wales." "For what?" "For the end."

BEDSIDE MANNER

RAWK'S POV

While I retrieved the suitcases from Oliver's police car another pulled up. "What's going on here? Who are you and where is Finch?" Both guys got out and walked toward me. I was beyond exhausted and just wanted to crawl into bed with Amarelia. "Finch was arrested a few hours ago." "That explains why he wasn't responding." One said to the other. "Wait did you say HE was arrested?" "Yeah turns out he's part of a fucked up cult and he's a rapist." I deadpanned

"No ways, Finch always seemed so down the line." The guys' badge said, Alberts. "Well he wasn't, he was way off the line. You'll hear all about it on the news I'm sure. A Detective Campbell from Scotland Yard will make contact but these are his details if you need to verify." I shoved a card at them and one took it.

Chloe walked up to ask if we were ready to leave, our ride needed to get back to Detective Campbell. The officers took one look at her and it confirmed what I was saying. "Did Oliver do that to you?" "Yes but this is nothing compared to what he did the last time. I know he's your fellow officer but I hope he fucking rots in hell." Chloe curled her lip in disgust and turned on her heel. "You are free to go."

Alberts clarified and we walked across to the waiting van.

I kept Amarelia as close as possible and when we got back to my car I only let go of her when absolutely necessary. I really didn't feel like going to the hospital but the quicker we did the quicker I could get her up to North Manor and to safety. The irony of the situation did not go unnoticed. I was taking her to the place I told her to never go.

I suggested Rhys take the girls to his, Chloe needed to get cleaned up and Amarelia looked overwhelmed. She shook her head as soon as the words left my mouth. "No." "No what?" "No Rawk I'm not going anywhere without you again." I was selfishly thrilled because truthfully, I wanted her with me. Her eyes darted desperately between mine and I nodded. "Okay if that's what you need." "Yes, it is." "I'll call you as soon as I have an idea of what's happening with him," I told Rhys before we drove off.

Amarelia was quiet. I could see the wheels spinning in her brain. "You alright? What's going on in that pretty head?" We were parked outside a McDonald's.Nneither of us had eaten all day.

"There's something I didn't tell anyone earlier." She muttered under her breath. "Why?" I tensed up "I wanted to tell you first, it's about Charlotte." I felt like I'd been punched in the gut. "What about my mother?" I tried to keep control of my voice.

"He had her killed, your father. He told me that I reminded him of her and he would make sure that I got the same grand exit that she did." She looked at me with such sorrow on her face but I was too stupefied to say anything. I swallowed hard.

"Grand exit?" "Apparently realistic car accidents were Aleksy's thing." I clenched every muscle I had to stop the fury I felt from overtaking me.

"I swear to you Amarelia my father will never see the light of day again, none of them will." I pulled her in close but she buried her face in her hands and wept. I let her, she had stayed calm and strong for long enough already." She mumbled something in between sobs but I couldn't catch it so I pulled her fingers away from her face slowly. "Please tell me, baby."

"He took my ring, your grandmother's ring. He said he'd add it to your mother's." She held up her bare hand and shivered. "That fucking cunt!" I slammed the steering wheel a couple of times before gaining composure. "You WILL have it back before we leave that hospital," I promised her but there was something else I could see it. "What else?" Her eyes darted between mine.

"There may still be video footage. Your father called Finch and told him to destroy it but I'm not certain how soon after that he was arrested." "Shit! I'm calling Nicky."

She'd done the absolute right thing. If Amarelia told Detective Campbell we'd be in a very different situation right now. North Manor would be crawling with cops. All of us would be sitting ducks.

Rawk called Nicky and between us we worked out where Connor may have hidden the evidence, they would search the house. We drove the rest of the way to the hospital in silence. Rawk was angry and sad and I didn't know what to do because he'd shut down on me. I knew he had a lot to process so I gave him the benefit of the doubt.

"Ready?" I slid my eyes over him and watched his jaw pop at the sides. "I love you Amarelia, even when I'm being a dickhead. I just, it's a lot and I don't know how to share it with you because I've never-" I put my finger to his lips and shook my head. "I know and it's okay I get it. Let's get this over with so we can go home." "And where's home?" He sniggered "Where ever you are Rawk." I kissed him softly and felt him slowly smile. "I fucking love you yeah."

We went into critical care and after speaking to Campbell we found the doctor and discussed transferring Connor to Wales. Then we were allowed to see him. I was actually relieved when we were told that a guard would have to be in the room with us. I wasn't sure if Rawk would keep his head.

"Can he hear me?" Rawk asked the nurse who was taking vitals from Connor. I chose to stay in the background. "He's conscious but he's on a high dose of morphine for the pain." Connor had been shot twice, once in the hip and again in the shoulder. Lucky for him the one to the hip went clean through and missed anything major. She left with a smile at the guard and closed the door behind her.

Rawk stood at his father's bedside and looked him up and down then shook his head. "The great Connor North reduced to nothing but a criminal." His father sputtered and coughed then tried to focus his eyes on Rawk. "What the fruck arr yoou doing here?" He slurred, panting slightly. "I came to get Amarelia's ring back and to let you know that I'll be getting my mother's one back too." He held my ring up and Connor sucked in air.

The machines connected to him beeped violently and the same nurse came rushing back in. "Calm down Mr North. I'm going to have to ask you to leave please." She frowned at Rawk before turning back to his father. "With pleasure." He snapped back and motioned me toward the door but turned as he went through. He knocked his fist on the door.

"Oh I forgot to congratulate you on bringing down the Elite Businessman's Club, I'm sure they'll be very appreciative." The machines went berserk as we walked away and I gripped Rawk's hand. "Shit's about to get rough. Don't let go yeah." He whispered with a smirk. "Never."

STICKS & STONES

NICOLE'S POV

"I'm sorry Chlo, one more time." My mobile was sticky against my cheek and I cringed when she swore under her breath at me but I had to find this for Rawk. I remember how he was before all this; before Carys and his ma even before Connor started becoming the twat he is now. Siobhan and I were neighbours when we were young and we remained friends through life.

"Darlin are you sure about this?" Stuart scratched his head and sized up the wall. I chuckled and squeezed both his shoulders. "Not even close but you got a better idea?" He blew air through his lips and shook his head. I passed him a hammer and stepped back. He slid ridiculous yellow goggles on and raised the tool above his head. Siobhan called just before he swung.

"Wait! It's not there. I think I know where it is. There's a hidden panel in the room next to this one. It used to be Aunt Charlotte's old craft room." She gestured for the door and we followed. After feeling her way around she called us over. "If I remember correctly you move this book. Rawk used to hide his chocolate in here and there should be a button-" She ran her fingers up and down and yelped when a section of wood panel moved aside to reveal a shelf.

"Holy shit! It's all here. What do we do?" She pulled files and USB sticks out and handed them to Stu. "We need to put all this in bags and hide it elsewhere until Rawk gets here," I answered and she bit her lip. "What?" Stuart asked her, we both knew what biting the lip meant. "It's just, don't you think the cops should have this as evidence? What if they say it's not usable because it's been tampered with."

"Rawk deserves to see that footage in private before anyone else Shiv." "Fuck yeah, your right I just can't believe all this is happening. Peter's mother won't stop calling me, I'm just a little stressed that's all." I hugged her into my side as we walked out. I knew she was riding her own rollercoaster of emotions.

"I need a drink." Siobhan sighed as we reached the kitchen. "Yes!" Stuart and I agreed. "First I'm dying for a fag though." He confessed and I grabbed my lighter. "Smoke on the patio." She called behind us. There is something about the first drag of a smoke after a stressful day. Nothing hits the spot quite like it.

"You alright darlin?" Stuart asked and I smiled widely. "I'm good babe, just a bit freaked out by all we've found out." "Yeah what type of people do you hang around with?" He teased and stepped into the space between us. His face turned serious then, "After this is sorted I'm done Nic, no more pretending." "I know Stu but the next while is going to be really hard on her, she needs us now more than ever." "Yeah and I need you." He pulled me into his arms and kissed me deeply.

RAWK'S POV

The thought of a four-hour drive did nothing for me so I told Rhys we'd be there first thing. They were almost at North Manor. We drove to a hotel in the centre of London. Amarelia ordered room service and took a shower while I spoke to my grandparents and Murray. Nicky called to say she found the evidence. So far they were all safe but I knew we couldn't let our guard down. Finch would get bail, he and Judge Coleman, and then we were all fair game.

"I'm so tired!" Amarelia yawned and dropped onto the bed. "Me too, come here." I opened my arms to her and she shuffled into my side. "How are you?" She whispered, kissing my bare chest. "You're safe and my father's going to jail so I'm good." "I'm sorry for everything that's happened. I know things are going to be difficult for you and your family but know that I'm here for you."

"As long as I have you beside me I can face anything." I kissed her head and felt her smile against my skin. "How's Siobhan holding up?" "Nicky thinks it hasn't hit her yet. Her father got dragged in for questioning. Aunt Sara and her are going in tomorrow."

"Whoa, what a mess." "Yeah, my father has a way of fucking up the lives of those around him." "You and Rhys have pretty much

stopped them though." She looked up at me with her huge chocolate eyes and my heart squeezed. I moved off the bed and dug in my jacket pocket then kneeled beside her.

"You're the full stop at the end of my sentence Amarelia. You make me mean something. You give me a beginning and an end. I can't wait to live through all of the middles with you." I picked up her hand and slid her ring back on. "I fucking love you." She said as she sat up and pulled me to kiss her.

She fell back and I hovered over her. "My father said that you remind him of my mother," I mumbled, I wasn't sure what I was trying to reassure her about but his comment had bugged me.

"He said I look similar to her." "You do and you don't. She had dark features like yours but it's not that. You have the same spirit as her. You're brave, kind, smart and an incredibly beautiful person. That's how you remind me of her." I rolled off her and onto my back. My arm covered my eyes. It still hurt to talk about my mother. The reality of her missing punched me anew each time.

"Rawk everything that I love about you was taught to you by your mother. I'm honoured to be compared to her in whatever capacity." She pulled my arm away from my head.

When I opened my eyes she smiled and leaned in to kiss me all over my face. "You're my home and you have my heart." I pulled her

onto me and wrapped my arms around her
waist. "I fucking love you."

We woke early, way too early for me. While I got dressed and calmed my dramatic mother down Rawk offered to get me coffee. I was glad he wasn't around to hear her rant. Granted I hadn't spoken to her in a few days but that wasn't unusual.

"I spoke to dad the other day, what's the problem mother?" "Aki told me you were there?" "Yes I was, I was there sent by the University for a project." I was now grateful for the lie. "Was your research partner also part of this project?" Her sarcasm oozed through the phone and I realised that in the bigger picture of my life she had become irrelevant." "No, he was there for me." "WHAT? I told you NOT to get involved with that boy." "Yeah well, I didn't listen did I?"

"You know how this is going to play out, don't you. He'll take what he wants from you and then he'll dump you and you'll be a mess again." "Wow, you are something else! I don't need your permission nor do I appreciate your opinion. Rawk is my future and if you don't like that then you don't have to be a part of it. I have to go." I didn't give her a chance to say anything before disconnecting the call.

I turned and Rawk was watching me with a fat smirk on his face. "What?" "You are so out of my league." He sauntered over to me and put my coffee down. Then his hands wrapped around my waist and he squeezed. "But I like your league." I pouted and he pulled me into a searing kiss.

We left the hotel and made our way to Cardiff via a visit to Detective Campbell. Rawk's father would be transferred in the evening if he remained stable. Finch and Judge Coleman made bail. Apparently, a fight broke out last night at the jail Oliver and Piotr are in. Both got the shit beat out of them. Rawk shot me a sly smirk at that news, Rhys had warned him. We got snacks and set off for North Manor.

WAITING IN WALES

"Hi, Nicole. We're about 10 minutes away." I sang on my phone when it rang. "It's Ian, the fuzz have pulled up and they wanna search the house. They're saying it's because of Connor's arrest but Nicky said to call because they're all Chief Finch's guys." "Shit!" I looked at Rawk with saucer eyes.

"Where's Rhys?" Rawk hissed. "They should be back any minute now. He and Siobhan have gone to get aunt Emily. She called about an hour ago in an absolute state." "Fuck! Tell your ma to tell them that unless they have a warrant from Detective Campbell they can fuck off." "Okay I will but please hurry." He begged quietly. "We'll be there in 5 Ian." Rawk clenched his steering wheel and sped up.

"When we arrived the cops had cleared off and Sara was trying to calm her distraught sister down. Rawk didn't even spare her a glance as we passed. He went straight to Rhys. "I've called Campbell and Murray. Campbell says he'll be here this afternoon with your father's transfer and Murray said he's sent a security detail to your grandparents."

"Good thinking. Where's Ian? He was a little freaked out on the phone." Rawk looked around. "A little, the kid is inhaling fags on the patio." Chloe chipped in as she gave me a quick hug. "I'll go check on him." "You wanna come help me get Siobhan calmed down? Everything seems to have finally hit her in a big way!" Chloe asked me, her eyebrows spiked in emphasis.

Siobhan was a bloody mess and nothing either of us said coaxed her out of her bedroom. Eventually, we gave up and went back to the kitchen. Stuart sat at the breakfast nook along with Rawk's two aunts. Emily stole ashamed glances at Chloe until I asked if anyone wanted to eat. Sara started apologising immediately.

"We'll prepare something if you'll try getting Siobhan to come down?" I squeezed her forearm and smiled softly. Emily sat there for a few seconds before she clicked that she'd be left alone with us then scurried behind her sister.

"You okay that she's here darlin?" Stuart asked Chloe under his breath and I made myself busy finding ingredients. "Yeah I mean I can't hold it against her that her stepson is a rapist and a sick cunt." "That's my girl." He kissed her forehead and the questions burned on my lips but it wasn't my place.

Ian, Rhys and Rawk joined us and soon we had a whole breakfast menu going. Sara came down to make a plate for Siobhan and Ian followed her back up with plates for her and Emily. Soon we were tucking in. "Oh my God, these bacon rolls are amazing!" Chloe complimented me and Rawk grinned. "She's got a thing for piggy buns." He winked, making me blush.

Siobhan refused to leave the house so an associate of Detective Campbell's came over and asked them questions. He seemed happy when Emily appeared and asked if she could do her interview with him instead of going to the police station. She turned to us before going into the parlour with the officer.

"I never believed it and in my heart. I don't believe my husband did either but I'll tell them anything they want to know. I'm so sorry Rawk." She didn't wait for a reply. She whipped back around and went in. After she was done she went straight upstairs, bypassing us in the lounge.

"Hello," I answered when my mobile rang. "Hi Lia, it's David how is your sister?" Yeah, so I had to lie to him too. "Hi David, she is doing much better thank you. What's up?" Why was he calling me? "Well funny story, I seem to have misplaced that USB with the files on for the new research." I could feel him cringing through the phone. It was very out of character for him to be careless.

"Oh no okay, not a problem I can email them to you?" "Yeah, that would work. Thanks, Lia I have no idea where I put that USB, I'm so embarrassed." "Hey you're doing me such a solid, it's the least I can do." "When do you need it by?" "We start new research on Wednesday." "Cool, I'll do it ASAP. Thanks again, David." I disconnected and Rawk's eyes followed me when I stood up.

"What's wrong?" "David lost the USB with all my files for Callen's new research so I'm gonna email them to him." "Do you have the files on your laptop or in a folder?" "They're on my laptop, why?" "Your laptop is back at the University." He reminded me.

"Doesn't matter, I can call maintenance and get them to-." I stopped when Rawk scrunched his face and shook his head. "What?" "I reinforced your door and I have the key on me." "Shit okay so um." "I'll have to go down to London." He rubbed his face and I walked up to him. "He only needs them for 2 days. We can go back tomorrow after your father had been transferred and Campbell is here." He didn't argue just nodded before stepping around me and going upstairs.

When he didn't come back down I excused myself and went up. "Hi," I said when he looked up from his iPad. Tears were streaming down his face. My heart twisted at the sight. "It's the footage. I wanted to watch it before I gave it to Campbell." I nodded "Would you like to be alone, I don't mind, I just wanted to check on you." He waited for me to look back up before patting the bed beside him

RAWK'S POV

"Aunt Sara this is Detective Campbell. He has a few questions than he can escort you to the hospital." I introduced them and noticed how Emily moved closer. I gave Campbell the evidence. I said I came across it last night when I was scratching around. He also knew

*that Amarelia and I needed to go back to
London. He was sending us in the back of a
squad car. I made sure that we all knew the
plan and that there would be extra security
around North Manor before we left.*

*The drive was a lot smoother and quicker
thanks to the blue lights and siren. Officer Dale
dropped us off outside Amarelia's dorm and
parked his car. He said he was going to check
out the surroundings and I was grateful. I
didn't relish the idea of staying on the
University grounds but I also couldn't expect
Officer Dale to drive us back immediately.*

*The dorms were quiet as most students would
be in a lecture or in the common room so we
made our way quickly. Amarelia's roommate
was obviously back judging from the pile of gift
bags and cards on the desk. "Shit Jen said she
was staying at her girlfriend's. How did she get
in?" "She must have gotten a locksmith."
Amarelia shrugged.*

*She grabbed her laptop and some bits then we
met Dale back at his car. I directed him to my
dorm and he said that after a quick bite he'd be
back to keep an eye on us from the parking. We
walked back to mine and I noticed the keyhole
had scratches all around it. Someone had tried
to get into my room.*

*While Amarelia sent off her emails and spoke
to Ari and her sister, I secured my door and
called Rhys. We ate the food Sara sent with us
and had a shower together than I pulled
Amarelia into me and fell asleep wrapped*

around her. Now we just had to get back to Wales without incident...

BUT BEFORE THAT

"Got everything?" Rawk pulled me into a kiss and I held onto him. It's a strange thing to say but amidst all the drama being alone with Rawk in his dormitory was like a holiday. "Yeah." I smiled up at his beautiful eyes. "Let's go find Officer Dale then."

He was talking on his mobile; looking a lot more awake then either of us when we got down to the parking. "Alright?" Rawk shook his hand "Good morning, Detective Campbell called to say I should get you two back up as soon as." We left University grounds and after a detour to McDonald's hit the road back to Cardiff.

We were barely through the front door when Nicole barrelled into us. "We need to talk!" She dragged us into the parlour and started pacing. "Nicky stop! What's up, what happened?" "Finch came here this morning. He said he had a few personal things to collect." "What the actual fuck, are you serious?" Rawk hissed. "Yeah but Siobhan's dad came down and fucked him off. Told him he'd crack his skull the next time he came anywhere near his family and that he was a disgrace."

"Holy shit!" I was shocked and impressed. "What happened?" Rawk asked quickly. "He didn't want to go at first but when Stu, Rhys and Ian came down so he backed off. I don't think it's the last we'll see of him though." "He wants the evidence. He probably thinks it's still here." "Of course, he wouldn't know that Lia

222

overheard and told you." I listened quietly but a plan was coming together in my head.

"I have an idea, it's risky but it would prove all of the charges against them." Before I could break my idea down someone came down the stairs two at a time. "Is my arsehole brother back Nicky?" "No, it's Rawk Uncle Colin." She replied as the guy came into view. "Rawk, oh my days how are you lad?"

"Good, how are you?" "Not that proud of my family name at the moment but we'll get to the bottom of all this." He scratched the back of his neck and grinned sheepishly then his eyes landed on me. "You must be Lia, pleased to meet you." He shook my hand and his eyes never left my face.

"I apologise for staring, you just remind me of someone." "Charlotte?" I asked quietly and he nodded sadly. "She was an angel, she didn't deserve Connor." He cleared his throat and asked if we'd eaten. "Actually we have something to discuss with everyone. Nicky would you mind getting them." Rawk asked, pulling me into his side. "I'll go. Siobhan and Sara are still asleep. Last night was a long and rough one." Colin said before walking out.

"Not to be a dick but can we trust him?" I asked uncertainly. "Before last night I would have said hell no but I was there when Rhys and Chloe explained everything to him. He was genuinely shocked. He had no idea and he wants nothing to do with any of them. When Campbell called Rhys last night Colin asked if

he would come over today to discuss the case."
"Okay, that's good."

We freshened up and caught up with the others until Siobhan came down with her mum and aunt in tow. "Jesus, she looks like shit!" Rawk whispered into my hair and I shot Nicole a sympathetic look. Chloe and Rhys came in from the patio behind Stuart and Ian.

"I have a proposition to put forward, a way to ensure that the guilty stay off the streets." I started once everyone sat. Emily raised her brows but no one said anything so I carried on. "Finch believes that the evidence Rawk handed over is still here. So what if we plant some evidence and a few microphones."

"Isn't that entrapment?" Colin asked. The front gate intercom chimed suddenly making all of us jump. "It's Campbell. Decide if we're all in on this or not because it will take everyone to pull this off yeah." Rawk's eyes dragged across each of us before he made his way to the door.

"Detective Campbell come in, Officer Dale, coffee?" Rawk led them into the kitchen and introduced them around. "We have an idea." I said, "But we need you to tell us if it's legal." Chloe cringed at her words. "And if it's possible." Nicole finished off and then we got down to details.

"You three are scary!" Campbell pointed between Chloe, Nicole and me with a grin. "Yeah, you girls should totally join the force." Dale teased.

RAWK'S POV

*The undercover cops that were watching Finch
and co. called to say they had definitely bought
into our lie. Colin took his family and Emily
home with a security detail following them.
Nicky and Stuart went back to his. Rhys and
Chloe went to his parents. They asked us to
join them but I didn't want to see Carys's
family so we stayed at North Manor.*

*"Oh my God, someone had best be fucking
dying. WHAT?" I grumbled to myself then
barked into my phone. It was too early.
Amarelia sat up beside me with saucer eyes.
"It's me, they're outside the house." Officer
Dale told me. "Sorry, thank you." I pulled
clothes on and Amarelia did the same then we
made our way to the safe room. That was the
condition Campbell had for us staying at North
Manor.*

*We watched on the monitor as the front door
opened and Finch pocketed a set of keys. The
fucker had keys to MY house. Guess we could
add theft as well as breaking and entering to
his rap sheet. He made his way straight
upstairs and toward my ma's art and supplies
room. It had long since been cleared out of any
memory of my mother. Finch knew exactly
where to go and soon he had his greedy little
fingers on the 'evidence'.*

*"There's someone else in the house Rawk."
Amarelia pointed at the hooded figure that
limped up the stairs to meet Finch. "Call Dale
and tell him to let Campbell know he needs*

225

backup." While she did that I turned back to the screen. When my eyes landed on Damon, walking through my front door with not a care, something snapped inside me.

I grabbed the mobile from Amarelia without warning. "Damon Coleman is here with Finch and another guy." "Shit okay, Campbell says back up is less than 5 minutes away." I disconnected before he finished and flung my phone onto the couch. Amarelia didn't say a word, only watched the screen. After a few moments, she looked up. "Motherfucker...that's Oliver Finch." She pointed at the guy who had just pulled his hood back and I saw red. Rage inducing, thought bypassing RED. I flung the safe room door open.

Amarelia's hand gripped my forearm. "Be careful Rawk they're dangerous and I don't want to lose you because of them." She didn't try to stop me or scream at me and for some reason that made me angrier. "Stay here yeah," I ordered her and she nodded. I made my way across the landing and stood at the door listening to their conversation. They truly believed they had found it before us, dumb fucks!

Finch told Oliver to go get the car while he and Damon did a final sweep of the house. I waited for them in my father's office. The layout of the room would give me the most advantage in a fight. Damon sauntered in and went through the drawers in the desk. He had Finch on speakerphone.

"Looks like North did a good job of clearing out. I'm surprised Rawk and Rhys didn't have cops crawling all over this place." "That little twat had no idea about any of it, not until he got that little girlfriend. Rhys and Chloe are to blame for this." "Little bitch, we should have helped her out the same way we did with Vicky." Damon chuckled.

I knocked the phone out of his hand as I tackled him from behind. I don't remember the next few minutes. I just released on him and didn't stop until I felt someone pull me back off him. I thought it was Dale or Campbell but it was Oliver. He pulled out a gun and told me to take a seat.

I heard a scream through Damon's phone and soon Finch came into the office, dragging Amarelia with him. He had a knife to her neck and she looked terrified. This was my fault. I never should have left her. "Hello, lad." He over-pronounced and lifted Amarelia up with an arm around her waist. She cringed and the knife's tip bit into her skin.

I swallowed and held my hands up. "Finch, what the hell are you doing? She has nothing to do with this, just let her leave and we can sort this out between us yeah." I tried to sound in control but on the inside, I was ripping all of them apart with my bare hands. "This little bitch ruined everything." "What the hell are you on about?" Where the fuck was Campbell with backup? I stood slowly and Oliver moved toward the door.

227

"Listen to what you're saying. How is that even possible?" I asked, taking a subtle step forward. Not subtle enough, Finch jerked and drops of blood ran down Amarelia's neck. "Don't move!" He warned "Sorry I won't move but listen to me yeah this is not gonna end well."

"For you two, no. For us, yes. See I started making my own plans when your father got sick. With him out of the way Oliver, Damon and I along with my brother, the honourable judge, had plans to take over Wales and the UK's underworld. The only thing I needed was for you to stay away long enough for him to die. His will would have been absorbed into North Enterprises of which I own a rather large portion and we would have been kings." If only he knew that my father didn't own North Enterprises anymore, my ma did.

He jerked again and this time she cried out. A line of blood appeared where the knife had slit. My blood ran cold and my knees buckled. "Amarelia!" I shouted and she sobbed aloud. Campbell appeared behind him and pressed a gun into Finch's neck. "I will cut off your neural pathways before you can slice her throat. Put the knife down."

Campbell's words had their effect and slowly Finch lowered his hand. Without notice, he launched Amarelia toward me and spun around to face Campbell. I screamed but it was too late, the detective crumpled to the floor. "Oh my God, he stabbed him!" Both of us slid over to Campbell's side.

"Campbell, Campbell can you hear me?" I shook him and suddenly his eyes opened then he coughed. "Arsehole!" He sat up and rubbed his side. Amarelia and I shared shocked expressions. "Bulletproof vest. I didn't become a detective without a few lessons learnt." We helped him up and went outside.

The driveway was packed with cop cars and I noticed a news van pulling up outside the gates. "The vultures are here, I nodded my head toward the gate and Campbell followed my eye. "Oh I know, I invited her. Best way to stop rats is to flush them out into the open. Officer Dale, please escort Mr Coleman's ambulance to the hospital." He grinned at us then waved the reporter through.

ON THE TELLY

"Jesus we're on the telly!" Nicole sent the plate on her lap flying as she stood. We were holed up at Stuart's. Campbell turned North Manor into a crime scene after arresting Oliver and Jack a week ago. Damon joined them once he was well enough to leave the hospital. Rawk was pissed and stressed but there wasn't much we could do about it. "You alright darlin?" Stu stuck his head through the doorway. "Call Rawk, oh my God, we're on the news!"

Rawk skidded into the lounge behind Stuart and we gawked at the huge screen. My mobile shrilled beside me a few seconds later. "Holy shit!" I launched at it then grimaced. "Who is it?" Rawk stuck his hand out and offered to answer for me. "My mother." He retracted his hand instantly and flexed his jaw. "You don't have to answer yeah." He told me gently. "She won't stop until I do." I sighed

"Hello, mother." I braced myself. "What. Is. Going. On. Lia, why is your face splashed across international news?" She hissed across the line. "I can explain." "Explain!? Explain I don't want you to explain I understand perfectly. I need you to get yourself on a flight and come home immediately. I warned you to stay away from that boy and now? Now you're part of a criminal investigation." I rolled my eyes and pinched the bridge of my nose.

"I'm not going anywhere mother. I'm right where I need to be." "WHAT? Amarelia Wolfe I am warning you, you best do as I say." "Or what mother? You'll disown me for embarrassing the family? I'm done with your threats, if you want to disown me then do it. Besides I can't leave, as you said I'm part of an investigation."

"I swear I will get on a plane and come fetch you myself. You are still my daughter and-." "AND WHAT? I said NO! I said I can't leave, I SAID I am where I want to be with whom I want. Goodbye mother." "If you put the phone down you can consider yourself no longer my daughter" "You already made that call when you told me it was my fault Joseph nearly killed me." I seethed and she had the audacity to gasp. Rawk took the phone and disconnected the call.

"I'm sorry baby." He pulled my shaking body against him and stroked my back. "I think I'm going to call it a night." I blinked frustrated tears away and stepped back. Nicole shot me a smile and Stuart made himself very busy cleaning the carpet. I could see Rawk wanted to argue but he nodded and said he'd be up soon.

RAWK'S POV

The phone call from Amarelia's mother wasn't the last. I spent hours fielding questions and concerns from both her phone and mine. Finally, I collapsed beside her. "I'm sorry Rawk." She whispered in the dark. "For what Amarelia? You have nothing to apologise for." I pulled her into my side. "I don't want you to ever think I regret my decision to be with you."

231

I don't know how she knew but the question was swirling around in the back of my head.

"I fucking love you yeah." I pulled her up to kiss me. She was warm and soft and gave way under my tongue. "I love you." She mumbled against my lips then dropped her head onto my chest. We talked for a while; about all that had happened and all that was to come. I told her that I had spoken to her siblings and father. They were a lot more understanding and calm than her mother.

"Morning, did you sleep at all?" Nicky queried when Amarelia dropped onto a stool beside her. "Yeah, a bit but Rawk and I spent hours talking everything through so I feel like I could sleep for a day or two." She yawned again. "I feel you, Rhys called at God knows what time and we were on the phone forever." She stretched and yawned. "Is everything okay? What did he want?" I asked.

"Morning all, hey darlin." Stuart rounded the breakfast nook and dropped a kiss on Nicky's head. I saw the momentary crease appear on Amarelia's forehead but she wiped it off before they saw. She was wondering about them and Siobhan but she would never ask. So I did,

"I know it's none of my business but what's the deal with you two and my cousin anyway?" They locked eyes then Nicky sighed. "Shivvy knew that she needed a cover at University. Peter was around and talks of marriage had started, all she needed was a guy to hit on her and for it to get back home. So Stu offered to

be her hedge." "Her hedge?" I asked, "Yeah you know how a hedge hides what's going on behind it." I nodded slowly.

"So you and Siobhan were never really together?" Amarelia asked. "Nope. I love the girl like a sister but she's a lot to handle and that's without the drinking problem." Stuart assured us. "Huh, that's wow you are a great friend to do that," Amarelia said absently and Stuart dismissed her with a hand flap.

"Not to change the subject but can we go back to Rhys calling?" I turned to Stuart and he relayed the conversation. "So we go to court tomorrow?" "Yeah, that's what Campbell told Rhys. We need to go to the station after breakfast to discuss everything. The rest will meet us there." Nicky finished off. "Guess this is really happening."

We were escorted through the station by Officer Dale and met a room full of people connected to the case. We would all have to stand trial. Chloe looked around nervously. "Hey, we'll all be there with you." I murmured and she gave a quick smile. After explaining how the day would run we were allowed to leave. Campbell called behind us, to hold on.

"You may return to North Manor, the investigation is complete and it is no longer a crime scene. Besides, I think it's the safest place for all of you. Officer Dale and his partner Pennyweather will be stationed on the property." "Is there reason for extra precautions?" I clipped out, what wasn't he

telling me? "Your father had to be put into solitary confinement for his own safety. There was an attempt on his life but no-one's speaking." I simply nodded, thanked the Detective and left. I felt nothing for my father but revolt. My people on the other hand had to be kept safe.

STATE YOUR NAME

If my mother thought I was an embarrassment before, nothing could have prepared her for the trial. It was a media frenzy. Everyone's dirty laundry was looked at under a microscope. The Elite Businessman's Club was pulled to pieces, members were subpoenaed and the depth of the club's reach was exposed. The girl's rapes took days to get through and so did Rawk's mother's murder. Aleksy was dead, which was unfortunate considering he had been the mastermind behind Charlotte's *'accident'*.

I woke up one morning to find Josef's face plastered all over the news along with the pictures from my hospital file. Rawk fumed down the line at the editor in chief of the publication. "That event has fuck all to do with this trial so I suggest you remove that story as well as those images...oh really well let me put it to you this way then. Take that shit down or I'll have our lawyers make sure you never publish another story again yeah. You have half an hour." He slammed the phone down and shook his head.

The trial was hard on all of us but for Siobhan, it was the opening to her free fall. All the pain and betrayal she had endured was dredged up for her to live through again. She wasn't coping and the night before her final day of questioning she got inebriated and had such a severe panic attack that she had to be hospitalized.

We sat shoulder to shoulder in the courtroom and watched Connor being dragged in. Oliver, Damon, Judge and Chief Finch as well as Piotr all sat behind their lawyer already. I noticed Rhys grinning at Oliver's bruised face and elbowed Chloe. She shrugged "Rhys promised him he'd get touched, a lot."

Connor was questioned last and made the most of his *failing health.* He coughed and wheezed worthy of an Oscar. "I have one last person to call your honour. I would like to call Mrs North to the stand." Connor and the Finches laughed and sniggered until I stood up and approached. Connor's face went slack then and Jack looked as though his head might pop off.

"Mrs North I have only 2 questions for you. First question, when did you two get married and second question, why?" I knew immediately what he was trying to do. He was trying to attack my character. Rhys had warned me that this may happen. "We were married on the 1st of January this year in Ireland." "Officially?" He asked, looking at the udge then at our defence. The judge raised his brows at our lawyer. "Yes of course. I have the paperwork here." He handed the marriage certificate over.

"And my second question Mrs North?" He seemed annoyed now. "You want to know why I married my husband?" My voice had a tinge of sarcasm in it that was impossible to miss. A few chuckles could be heard from the gallery. "Well it's a good question, you hardly know him and now you're married. Seems convenient." "For whom?" I scoffed.

"Answer the question please Mrs North and there better be a point to this line of questioning Mr Grady." The judge warned. "I married Rawk because I love him." "Huh, so it has nothing to do with the fortune he stands to gain if he marries before his father dies." The lawyer smirked. He thought he'd caught me out. I looked at Jack Finch and smiled innocently.

"Mr Grady Rawk asked me to marry him before we found out that his father was transferring the family fortune into his late wife's name to evade both the government and the Elites. Before we knew that, if he wasn't married prior to his father's death, everything would go to North Enterprises. And definitely before we found out that Chief Finch owns the majority share in NE." Connor had not been present when Jack was on trial.

Connor's head whipped around to face Finch. "You mother fucker!" He gripped Finch's arm but they were broken apart by guards. "Order!" The judge hit his gavel and shouted. "What is the point of these questions, Mr Grady?" "I think that they are in cahoots for the money and the marriage isn't real." "I assure you the only thing of any value to us in that entire portfolio is his mother's farm, Mr Grady." The lawyer looked flabbergasted and said he had no further questions.

He took his seat and immediately began whispering to Jack. Connor looked like he was ready to murder Finch. The day came to an end and the guards were told to remove the accused. "I would love to be a fly in that prison tonight," Chloe whispered to me as Jack and Connor were made to stand. Both were glaring at us as they passed. Connor narrowed his eyes at me as he passed,

"He will ruin you like he ruined Carys." He spat at me. The guard twisted his arm and he winced in pain. "Carys was ruined by your people, not mine." I shot back. "Move." The guard ordered shoving Connor forward. Beside me, Rawk was breathing in shallow pants. "Don't let him win, if you lose your shit he wins." He was about to argue when we heard screaming coming from the door Connor had just walked through.

Connor's guard ran back into the courtroom. "We need backup and medics! The accused were ambushed." He told the officers and guards still present. His uniform had blood splatter down the arm and his hands were drenched.

Two pledge members from the Elites managed to get guards uniforms. They were waiting in the hallway where all the accused were led down before being taken back to jail. The attack was over before it began. Judge Finch and Piotr were dead, along with one of the hitmen. The rest weren't far off and had to be rushed to the hospital. Oliver and Damon were in critical care but Connor didn't make it. He died in the ambulance on the way.

It was weird after. There was no way we could go back to North Manor. The reporters took up residence outside so we decided to visit Rawk's grandparents in France. That was... interesting. The French reporters were just as persistent and after 3 days of being followed around, we came back to Wales.

Rawk called Rhys and Nicole, we were all meeting at North Manor for dinner. He spoke to Sara and got her to get things organised. She told him that Siobhan agreed to go to a rehabilitation centre after the trial and Emily had filed for divorce. Damon was something they couldn't get past.

"It's good to get away from our fishbowl." Chloe patted my hand while we collected the cutlery to dress the table. Nicole was swearing at the napkins but stopped and grinned when we approached. "What?" I asked hesitantly. "You never had a wedding reception." She smirked. "So?" "You will regret not having one when your kids ask to see pictures one day." She hit me in the feels and my face fell for a moment.

"I was going to discuss it with my wife first but since Nicky has no chill...What do you think about having a party at the farm?" He asked me and my smile pinched at the corners. "I'd love that," I said before launching myself into his

open arms. "I fucking love you yeah."
We managed to get the girls calmed down by dessert so that we could tell them the real reason why we had asked them all over in the first place.

"Are you serious?" Rhys checked. "One hundred percent certain. Amarelia suggested it to my nan and she loves the idea." "So will she come over and run it as a dance school?" Chloe asked. "Planning on reigniting your ballet dreams Chlo?" Rawk teased. "That's a firm no but I do have another suggestion for North Manor. It would make an AMAZING gallery or showcase venue."

"It actually would. You should speak to Adaline when she gets here." Rhys suggested. "She hasn't decided what she wants to do but she'll be here in a few days." Rawk smiled absently then looked at Rhys, "How would you feel about coming to work for North Enterprises?" "Are you fucking serious?" Rhys dropped his spoon in his ice cream, he was stunned.

"I mean we're gonna need someone on retainer and I trust you, so?" "Yes oh man that's a yes!" Rhys high fived Rawk then pulled him into a fierce hug that had all of us giggling. "Nicole I suggested you come to the meeting with Adeline also." "Me, why?"

"So you can show her your incredible design and makeup skills, Miss Evers. I think you and Blanca would make a killer team." Amarelia grinned widely. "She showed my nan the pictures from the Profs Dinner." Rawk tugged me back into his lap and held me close. I was so happy and in love, the drama was over and we were all safe. The idea of celebrating our love on his mother's farm thrilled me.

FARM FANCY

RAWK'S POV

The girls went into full-on crazed planning mode. Nicky and Stuart were granted a special pardon during the trial. They'd been allowed to work via correspondence but afterwards had to get back to University to finish the year. She came up at every opportunity though and was thrilled to tell Blanca about the North Manor possibilities. Adaline Guillem was not one to shy away from taking an idea and running with it. Her and my grandfather came and stayed in Wales, meeting different people and indulging my wife.

"You have made your grandmother a very happy woman Rawk, thank you." He squeezed my shoulder as we watched her and Amarelia chatter away. "I think that's my wife's doing not mine." I smiled every time I said the words aloud. She was my wife.

"I have something for you." He smiled quickly but hesitated. He tapped his finger 3 times on the table. I have seen him perform this ritual all my life. He was uncertain about something. He shot me another look then said he'd be back.

He reappeared with a small velvet pouch. "This was the first piece of jewellery your grandmother and I bought Charlotte. She never took it off and was inconsolable when she believed she'd lost it." His fingers shook slightly as he held up a chain with a diamond star hanging off it.

"But you have it?" I didn't understand. My grandfather's breath hitched and his eyes shone. "One of the ushers found it at the opera house. They all knew who it belonged to and it was given back to Adaline. It was your mother's last birthday in Paris before she moved to the UK permanently to marry Connor. You chose well son, she will be your shining star just as your mama was mine."

"To be honest I don't think I ever had a choice in it, I literally fell for her the first day and I've been falling ever since." I held the jewel in my palm and battled the waves of sadness/joy that washed through me. "Long may it last!" He looked at my nan with such adoration and I prayed we would stand the test of time as well as they have.

"She's here she's here!!" Chloe screamed from the kitchen when Ari and Kit pulled up. Akia and Leila followed right behind Amarelia as they squealed and hugged them then cooed at baby Addison. Soon we found ourselves at North Manor, getting them settled into the guest room alongside Kit's parents and Amarelia's family.

My grandmother finally made up her mind and the result is THE hottest place to be seen. An exclusive venue that has seen some of the most exciting exhibitions and shows take place between its walls. She hired Nicky and Blanca as in-house set and styling consultants and they love it.

Kit's father, James, designed the new additions to North Manor. His mother, Sophia, took care of the landscaping and Murray improved the security. All this meant that Kit and Ari had become firm friends.

Rhys helped me pull North Enterprises onto the straight and narrow. Chloe kept a handle on the offices, I trusted her to manage problems and report back to me. She ruled with little patience for incompetence and was well respected.

I sold or cut ties with a lot of people I didn't want to associate with. And the best part of the last, almost, year... Amarelia and I moved onto the farm and later today we were going to celebrate our love with all of the people we love.

"Ready?" Akia asked she and Leila wore matching grins. "You two are as bad as gran. Remember that we've been married for almost a year already?" "Yeah yeah yeah but the farm looks amazing and you look amazing. I'm just so happy for you Ami wami. I thought for a while after Josef-." She swallowed hard and swiped a stray tear away.

Leila squeezed her hand and I pulled her into a hug. "I love you, both of you. Let's go do this before I mess my makeup and Blanca kills me." "I would NOT mess with her, after you," Leila whispered as we moved down the stairs of the farmhouse.

"It's not often that you get to marry the same couple twice but here we are," Rhys told the crowd. Chuckles and cheers went up around us. "Rawk and Lia would like to say a few words before we get this party started." He continued with a huge grin. I looked up into my husband's perfect face and felt overwhelming love.

"Bumping into you was the best thing that ever happened to me. Loving you is the best feeling that I've ever felt. Agreeing to spend the rest of my days getting to know you is the best decision I will ever make. Our love is the whole and we are the parts. I love you." I smiled through my tears, I was feeling so emotional.

Rawk took a deep breath and stepped toward me. He pulled a thin chain with a gorgeous star-shaped diamond pendant out of his breast pocket. Then he turned me toward our guests and put it on me. He turned me back to face him but stayed in close.

His hands came up to cradle my face and he dropped his head to mine. "Before I met you I was an island in the dark but you found me and you coaxed me and before I knew what was happening I was in love. You are my shining

star, the light that will always lead me home."
And then he kissed me.

RAWK'S POV

I kissed Amarelia with every bit of love I had in me. Every scrap she'd tended and grown. Her beautiful eyes swam and she whispered into my ear. I shot my head back and held her at arm's length. "You're pregnant? The words came out much louder than I'd anticipated and there was pin-drop silence around us for a few seconds before everyone started cheering with gusto.

"Yeah, times two." She answered with a smirk and waved two fingers before me. "As in twins?" I could feel my heart in my throat. "Pie and Sky." She teased and I scooped her into my arms and spun her around, kissing her. "I fucking love you yeah."

"Ladies and gentlemen Mr and Mrs North," Rhys said behind us suddenly making everyone laugh and clap. Soon after, the party moved to the tents. The scene was perfect, Amarelia didn't want OTT. She said farm fancy was good enough. Sophia and Aunt Sara got it exactly right. Hundreds of candles and fairy lights illuminated the trees and mirrored chandeliers created constellations under the tents.

Long after all our guests were tucked away in bed at North Manor Amarelia and I danced under the twinkling trees. The smile hadn't left her face for a second of the party and I was lost in a loop of realising we were going to be parents and feeling giddy all over again. "What's going on in that beautiful head of yours?" I tipped her chin up and she eyed me for a few seconds.

"Thank you for choosing me. Through all the shit and all the chaos you never once let me go so thank you." She kissed my fingers and I tugged her closer, circling my arms around her. "You were my only choice Amarelia. I'll never let you go. You're my person."

OPPOSITES ATTRACT

"Oh, Sky you scared the crap out of me! Hello baby. Go wake your brother and sister up." I kissed her head and grinned to myself as she snuck into Sebastian's room first. I couldn't wait for Stella and Dominic to arrive. Rawk was at the airport collecting them while I tried to get the farm organised for the day.

Contrary to what I claim I love being awake in the quiet of the early morning. Over the years I've come to appreciate silence. I guess three kids and a working farm will do that to you not to mention all Rawk's business as well. "Piss off Sky, I'm sleeping yeah." Sebastian groaned, he's just like his father, big and moody, but under that gruff exterior is a heart of gold.

He was due to start his first year at the Bristol Veterinary School in the fall. I always knew he would do something related, even as a young boy he loved nothing more than being with the animals on the farm. At the last minute, he decided to push it back and take a gap year instead. He came stumbling out of his bedroom still half-dazed and I laughed at the sight. He was such a grumpy bear when he didn't get enough sleep.

He and Charlotte stayed up until God knows what time getting things ready for the Dominic and Stella. The crossover of kids visiting has been happening for years, our families are all wonderfully close. Rawk and I will never be able to repay Murray for all he did. Ari and I like to hope that one day at least one set of our kids will end up in love.

"Mum seriously tell Sky to get lost!" Charlotte shrieked from her bedroom making Sebastian grin. "Charlie get your lazy ass up if dad gets back and you're still in bed he's gonna make you muck out the stables again," Sebastian yelled back. After a loud sigh, a lot of shuffling and a few thumps she emerged.

"And you can get lost now Sky, go find Pie, go on." She opened the door for the huge husky then came to rest her head on my shoulder. "Hi, mama." "Hey baby, want some eggs?" "I love you." She gave me her biggest smile and I heard Sebastian snort. "Oi don't hate the player, hate the game mate." She teased.

Pie and Sky's loud howls and yelps only meant one thing. "They're here!" Char clapped her hands and bounced around. Rawk walked in and swung me into a kiss, earning him a round of gagging sounds. "LIA!!" Stella ran straight into my arms and I hugged her tightly. Dominic shook his head choosing to plant a kiss on my cheek instead of all the fuss his twin made. He was so much quieter than his sister. Much more like Selene in that way.

Talk of the devil and in she walked, Pie following her as always. "Hey guys, how was the flight?" She asked quietly. I could see how tired she looked. "Sel your hair! You look amazing. Doesn't she look amazing Nic?" I watched the exchange with interest. She rolled her eyes when she noticed Stella and me both grinning at an obviously embarrassed Dominic. "Selene is beautiful with light or dark hair." He answered quietly.

Stella squealed beside me and Selene rolled her eyes again. "Oh my God, mum seriously! I need to shower, I stink from dancing." She mumbled but didn't leave. Instead, she made her way over to Dominic and picked up his coffee, sipping from it.

"So what do you lot wanna do today. Selene, Carys and Finley have the regatta tomorrow so I doubt they'll be joining us?" Rawk asked and the other three started talking at once while Dominic's eyes followed Selene's movements. Stella's voice stood out over the rest. "I haven't been on a horse since we were last here." "Hell to the no, thanks but I don't wanna smell like a farm." Charlotte sniffed.

"Guess it's just us then." Sebastian winked and Rawk elbowed him in the ribs. "Behave." "Ewww dad seriously she's like my older sister. No offence El." "None is taken and ditto." "Nic you want breakfast hun? Oh, and your room is all set up if you wanna crash for a bit." I offered him. He's such a gorgeous boy. I mean they all are, how could they not be with parents like Kit and Ari but Dominic looked most like his beautiful mother.

"Thanks, Lia I'll just freshen up quick, I'd love some real food please." He carried his suitcase and himself off down the passage. Stella and Sebastian were heading out already. "El what about breakfast?" "Ma do you know the girl at

250

all, I bet you had *Greggs* as soon as you landed yeah." "Damn straight." She shrugged and they were out the door laughing. She has an unhealthy obsession with sausage rolls

"So sad that those two don't see how perfect they are for each other," Charlotte commented with a sigh and I nodded. "What? Seb is far too moody for El." Selene snorted from behind her claimed coffee as she sat down beside her sister. "But that's why they'd work Sel, opposites attract." Charlie patted her hand. I didn't miss Selene's eyes looking to Dominic's door when the comment was made.

At breakfast, Dominic slid into the seat opposite Selene and started discussing his upcoming kickboxing fight with Rawk. It was such a relief that he was back in the octagon after Kelly's death. Kit tried to get Rawk into MMA, claiming that he was built for it but my husband is definitely more of a lover than a fighter. We ate and caught up before Rawk had to leave for North Enterprises. Charlotte had a day of shopping planned with her friend Lucy so she bummed a lift.

Later Rawk and I were having a drink with Chloe. She stopped over to drop off reports from the office and Carys's gear for the regatta. Even though Selene had never rowed a day in her life she enjoyed the event planning and structure of the sport and took it upon herself to be in control many years ago. As we sat surrounded by friends and family a warm feeling of contentment flowed over me.

"I fucking love you yeah." Rawk whispered into my ear and I melted. After all this time he still had the ability. "I fucking love you too." I kissed him but we were cut off by coughing and throat clearing. "Eww get a room, there are children present," Selene whined while covering Charlotte's eyes.

NEXT GENERATION

RAWK'S POV

"Surprise!!!" I know that voice... "Arialena is that you?" "IT'S THEM, aaahhhhh you made it!!!" Amarelia turned to me with Ari squashed tight against her. She looked so happy and it still felt like a privilege to share a part in that with her. A throat cleared and we all turned back to the door.

"Oh my God, Aki?" Amarelia squealed and ran into her sister's hug. "How?" She asked squeezing her then saw Leila and pulling her in too. The door opened and shut once more and Rhys walked in. His 15-year-old daughter, Carys, followed behind him. After a shy greeting, she bolted upstairs to Charlotte's room.

"Was she surprised?" Rhys asked me and I nodded slowly. A sly grin formed on my face. "You knew about Aki and Leila? And you kept the secret!?" "To be fair I only told him yesterday. I know he can't keep anything from you. I had business in the State's and open seats on the company plane." Rhys defended me and I knew from the look on Amarelia's face she was thinking of my need to 'work late' last night.

"Are you all coming to the regatta?" Selene asked from the stairs. Her eyes were like saucers and her brows were raised. "YES!"

The entire room answered before carrying on with their conversations. I watch her toe tap and wondered what was up. I know Selene and something was bothering her.

"We'll leave soon baby, you alright?" I asked, not going to her like I usually would. I know how much she hates being cornered when she's in a mood. She gets it from me. She looked up with a tight smile. "Yeah daddy I'm fine. Just...a guy from another school has been giving Lucy Sanders trouble and they're all gonna be there today." She whispered. "Okay and?" I ask and wait. She hates being forced to talk, again a wonderful trait passed down from me I guess.

"Please keep Seb away. I don't want him to get involved and get in trouble." She frowned deeply and looked so much like her mother it was incredible. "Baby are we talking about the same Sebastian. Your Dr Doolittle brother doesn't have a violent bone in his body."

I heard a quiet snort then Dominic appeared behind her on the stairs. "Well, we both know that's a lie. I'll break both Luke's wrists if he comes near you or Lucy." He mumbled just loud enough for me to catch. They stared each other down as he passed her and as soon as their eye contact broke his face morphed into a scowl. I narrowed my eyes at Selene but she turned taking the stairs two at a time.

"Morning Mr North." A line of girls chorused when I walked past with Finley and Carys's bags. "Hello girls." I smiled at my daughter's

teammates and they blushed as a group. "Daddy please don't make it any worse. They already drool over you, it's gross." She admonished under her breath but I saw the humour in her eyes. "I can't help it, baby, I was made to be adored." She just rolled her eyes again. "Need help?" Dominic appeared beside us and I handed him a bag. "Before she rolls her eyes into another dimension."

I left them to it and went to find my wife. After all these years it still gave me a thrill to say that. Rhys caught my attention and pointed beside him. Nicky and Stuart waved from beside Kit at the riverside, their son, Finley, was Captain of the boy's open team. I joined them and soon the regatta began. I watched Selene checking off lists furiously and chuckled, she was such a control freak. I looked around and couldn't believe this was my life. I looked down at Amarelia and she smiled up at me. "I fucking love you yeah."

DOMINIC'S POV

"What the hell...Selene don't?" I heard Finley up ahead and immediately I was moving. When I reached the clearing she was stood in front of Charlotte's friend, shielding her, from a guy who was twice her size. I felt blind rage pulse through me. Fin was trying to pull the boy back when I walked into it. "Fuck off mate this has fuck all to do with you. Now stop being an idiot Sel and move outta my way." That had to be the Luke Selene told me about. "No Luke just leave her be. She said it's over."

She replied quietly and for once I wished she wasn't so fucking brave.

Lucy peeped over Sel's shoulder and nodded her head. "I-I t-told you Luke we are over. Just leave me alone." Her voice wobbled dangerously, she was scared. I was scared too but not for her for Luke. I was going to fucking end him if he put even a finger on either of them. Selene looked furious and both our fathers had just appeared.

Instead of doing the logical thing the dickhead did the total opposite. He tried to reach around and grab Lucy. She ducked behind Selene and he lunged. I tried to get to her in time, to move her out the way but I was too late. Luke's fist collided with Selene's mouth. I heard Rawk and my dad swear simultaneously somewhere behind me.

It was all background, he'd split her lip. My vision tinged around the edges. I tried to calm down while I held her against me and watched her eyes swim back onto focus. She has the biggest eyes I've ever seen and I've been in love with them for months now. Even though I knew nothing would ever come of it. "Hey." She mumbled then hissed from the pain. "I'm sorry I didn't reach you in time, *tesoro*."

I gently wiped the blood off her lip with my thumb and her eyes pooled. It ripped my heart out. "I just wanna go home, Dom. Is Lucy okay?" "Yeah, she's fine. Your dad is freaking out though." I nodded toward Rawk who looked like he wanted to smash Luke into pieces while the dickhead tried to explain.

He practically swatted Luke aside to get to Selene. "Baby are you okay, I'm going to kill that little shit." And I didn't doubt for a second that he was capable. "Daddy please let's just go home." She pleaded. "Sel I am so sorry." Luke attempted an apology but the look I gave him stopped him in his tracks.

"Seb!" "Sebastian no wait." I heard El and Char call behind him but it was lost. He stormed up to Luke and pushed him away from Rawk. "Sorry dad, did I not tell you to stay the fuck away from Lucy the last time? She does not want to be your girl any longer. Now you've hurt my sister. Give me one good reason not to hurt you." Sebastian's temper was barely controlled. His father looked shocked, Seb was usually very good at remaining calm.

Luke tried explaining again but Seb cut him off. "You're lucky the coach and all these people are here right now or I would beat the shit out of you and then I'd let Dominic break what's left. I know he wants to, especially now." Selene went over to her brother and squeezed his arm. "It's not worth it Seb, leave it. The coach will take care of him."

Finley stood alongside Carys beside Sebastian. Seb's arm was wrapped around Lucy's waist. I had Selene tucked into my side and Charlie linked arms with Stella. "The next time you come near any of my people again you won't be walking away," Sebastian warned, pulling Lucy in tighter. "And don't even breath in Selene's direction, got it," I added. Luke just nodded repeatedly with his hands up.

RAWK'S POV

"Did you see Finley and Carys holding hands?" Rhys asked as we loaded stuff into various cars after the regatta drama was over. I smirked because I had noticed, "You're screwed now. It's all over." I teased him but he coughed "I also noticed Selene standing dangerously close to Dominic." I had to give it to him. "How did this happen Rhys, we were in our 20s and now we're worrying about our girls? "I know brother, I know." He chuckled.

Truth be told, if Selene ended up with a guy like Dominic Forrester one day I wouldn't mind. I saw the look in his eyes when Luke tried to speak to her. It's the same look I get when anyone looks at Amarelia wrong. I guess they're the next generation of lovers. And if our children are anything like us once they've found their person they'll never let go.

Printed in Great Britain
by Amazon

73029684R00147